The Lady Grace
Mysteries

From the Daybookes
of Lady Grace Cavendish

Book the First

Assassin

The Lady Grace Mysteries from Delacorte Press

ASSASSIN
BETRAYAL

THE Lady Grace MYSTERIES

From the Daybookes of Lady Grace Cavendish

BOOK THE FIRST

ASSASSIN

Patricia Finney is writing as Grace Cavendish

DELACORTE PRESS

Published by
Delacorte Press
an imprint of
Random House Children's Books
a division of Random House, Inc.
New York

Series created by Working Partners Ltd.
Text copyright © 2004 by Working Partners Ltd.

Visit us on the Web! www.randomhouse.com/kids
Educators and librarians, for a variety of teaching tools, visit us at
www.randomhouse.com/teachers

Library of Congress Cataloging-in-Publication Data
Cavendish, Grace.
Assassin / Patricia Finney is writing as Grace Cavendish.
p. cm.—(The Lady Grace mysteries, from the daybookes of Lady Grace Cavendish :
book the first)
Summary: Thirteen-year-old Lady Grace Cavendish, favorite maid of honor of
Elizabeth I, must solve a murder mystery and clear the name of her betrothed.
ISBN 0-385-73151-5 (trade) — ISBN 0-385-90189-5 (GLB)
[1. Kings, queens, rulers, etc.—Fiction. 2. Great Britain—History—Elizabeth,
1558–1603—Fiction. 3. Poisons—Fiction. 4. Diaries—Fiction. 5. Mystery and
detective stories.] I. Title PZ7.F49825As 2004 [Fic]—dc22
200302055

The text of this book is set in 13-point Cloister.
Book design by Trish Parcell Watts
Printed in the United States of America
September 2004
10 9 8 7 6   BVG

To Meg, with many thanks

MOST PRIVY AND SECRETE

THE DAYBOOKE OF MY LADY GRACE CAVENDISH,

MAID OF HONOUR TO HER GRACIOUS MAJESTY

QUEEN ELIZABETH I OF THAT NAME

LYING AT THE EASTERN CORNER,

THE MAIDS OF HONOUR, THEIR CHAMBER,

UPPER PASSAGEWAY,

WHITEHALL PALACE,

WESTMINSTER,

MIDDLESEX,

GOD'S OWN CHOSEN KINGDOM OF ENGLAND

Assassin

I am supposed to use this book to write all my prayers and meditations in. That's what Mrs. Champernowne said when she gave it to me for my New Year's Gift—and that I could make one of my beautiful embroideries for its cover, which I shall do, because I like making pictures with stitches. But why should I drone on like Lady Hoby about Improving Passages and Sorrowful Meditations on my sins? How boring!

Anyway, I don't commit any very terrible sins, apart from once ruining my gown when I jumped off a log. And losing things. That's why I haven't written anything in this before—I lost it under my bed for a while. But now I've found it I'm going to write everything in it. It can be a book about me, Lady Grace Cavendish, Maid of Honour. And all my favourite things. Why not?

My favourite person (apart from my mother, who is dead, God rest her soul) is Her Majesty the Queen. She's a bit old, which you're never supposed to say or she might throw a shoe at you. She is thirty-six! Even for a great lady, that is almost too old to get married and have children—as Mrs. Champernowne complains when she thinks nobody is listening. I think Mrs. Champernowne's pate is addled: why would a queen want to marry and gain a king she'd have to obey? In fact, why would anyone want to get married if they didn't have to?

Unfortunately, I have to. The Queen says so.

The most exciting day of my life is probably tomorrow. The Queen's Majesty has arranged a St. Valentine's Ball and I must choose one of the three suitors the Queen has selected for me, to be my wedded husband. We'll be handfasted once the lawyers have finished the contracts, and then I shall marry whoever it is properly when I'm sixteen. All three suitors are now at Court, ready for tomorrow.

I wish I didn't have to marry. I feel far too young to do so but, being an heiress, I must—though if I were a commoner I could wait until I was as old as five and twenty!

Mary Shelton just came in and made moan to me

about Lady Sarah not wanting to walk the dogs—
even though it is her turn. I see an opportunity. I
must run!

Later this Day

I am writing this in bed because Lady Sarah and
Mary Shelton aren't here yet and I cannot sleep.

My favourite place in all of Whitehall Palace is
behind the compost heaps at the end of the
Orchard. I must have a care when I go there
because if the other Maids of Honour or Ladies-in-
Waiting knew about it, they'd tell the Mistress of
the Maids, Mrs. Champernowne. And then she
would tell the Queen, and Her Majesty would have
to know about it officially, instead of just unofficially
as she does now.

So when I want to go there, I generally volunteer
to take the Queen's little dogs for a walk. Everyone
knows I'm the only one of the Queen's
Gentlewomen who actually likes them. They're
small and hairy and smelly and quite fierce and a bit
snappy if they don't know you—but I never have any
trouble with them. They like me.

That was why I had to stop writing earlier: I had

to run downstairs and find (my very pretty Lady and doesn't she know it?) Sarah Bartelmy. She was standing by the door to the Privy Garden with her face as sour as week-old milk, because *she* had been told to walk the dogs.

"What is wrong?" I asked, though I knew because Mary Shelton had told me.

Lady Sarah tossed her shiny copper hair and sighed. "The Queen bade me walk her dogs."

"Oh, what fun!" I declared, knowing she wouldn't agree. We play this charade with great regularity.

"But the wind is raw and there's a frost upon it," she complained. "And my mother sent me rose-water and almond oil to see if that will help my spot, and now I'll not have time to try it!"

Lady Sarah does have a spot on her nose, but it's not that big. She makes such a fuss about spots.

"Please don't trouble yourself. I will take the dogs out for you," I said kindly. "You must look your best for the ball."

For a moment Lady Sarah smiled at me quite pleasantly. Only for a moment, though. "I suppose you like galloping around with the horrible smelly little creatures," she observed.

"Yes, I do," I agreed. "Wait here, I'll get changed."

I ran up to our bedchamber—I share it with Lady Sarah and Mary Shelton—to change into my old green woollen hunting kirtle that's a bit short for me now. I couldn't walk the dogs in my white damask bodice and kirtle with the false front embroidered with roses. It was embroidered by my dear mother and is precious.

I didn't bother the tiring woman to help me—I can do it myself since I have all my bodices lacing up the front. I left my damask on the bed because I was in a desperate hurry to get out in the Orchard before it started getting dark. I pulled my boots on, grabbed my cloak, then rushed back downstairs again.

This time Mrs. Champernowne caught me on the back stairs. I think she lies in wait for me. "Lady Grace!" she shouted. "Lady Grace! Stop at once and wait!"

She's Welsh, you know, and very strict. But I have to be respectful to her, because she's served the Queen longer than anyone else—since Her Majesty was just Princess Elizabeth and everyone thought she'd be executed. So I stopped and curtsied. I knew exactly what she was going to say. And she did.

"Lady Grace! When will you live up to the pretty name your poor mama gave you? How many times do I have to tell you not to clatter down the stairs like a herd of cattle?"

Silly old moo, as if cows could run downstairs.

"Sorry, Mrs. Champernowne," I said meekly, though I wasn't sorry because I *don't* clatter. I was going as quietly as I could and it's not my fault my outdoor boots have hobnails in them.

"Now walk, child, look dignified. What would the Queen say if she saw you like this? Why cannot you be more like Lady Sarah?"

Oh yes, be like Lady Sarah Copper-locks Bartelmy and squeal every time I see a spider and have nothing in my head except how white my skin is and how shiny my hair is and whether some idiotic young gentleman is writing stupid sonnets to my chest. Hah!

I didn't say that, though it was a struggle. I said, "Yes, Mistress Champernowne." And curtsied again and walked as gracefully as I could with my knees bent, so she wouldn't spot just how too short my old kirtle is and make me go and change again. Then once I was round the corner I ran even faster to make up for lost time.

I came puffing out into the Queen's Privy Garden, which is all formal and deadly dull. Lady Sarah was standing under a tree, her face covered with a scarf to protect her complexion, scowling at Henri, who was lifting his leg against one of the roots.

"What took you so long?" she sniffed.

"Mrs. Champernowne caught me running and told me to be graceful like you." I said this with a straight face so she couldn't be sure whether I was being sarcastic or not. Though I'm not sure Lady Sarah Bartelmy actually knows what sarcasm is.

She sniffed again, gave me the leash, and hurried off back to the palace before the cold air could damage her white skin any more.

I kept the dogs on the leash in the Privy Garden so that they couldn't go digging up hedges from the maze as they did last time. They were so happy to see me; they were barking and bouncing round me and bringing me interesting sticks. I walked as sedately as I could down the path, past the big fountain that was still frozen, and on to the gate into the Orchard.

One of the Queen's Guard was there, guarding the gate from ferocious apples probably. He was looking miserable, his nose bright red and dripping from a cold. It was his own fault: he was too vain to put on his cloak and hide his wonderful crimson doublet and puffed velvet hose, and his white stocking hose on his handsome legs and his smart, polished high boots. I expect he was hoping Lady Sarah would walk past him, or maybe that the Queen would come by and admire how handsome he is—all the gentlemen hope for that.

"Will you open for me, sir?" I asked with a curtsy.

He sighed, turned the key, and opened the gate. He didn't even bow! He would have for Lady Sarah, I believe, if only to get in a stare at her dugs. Not for me, though. My body hasn't started to develop in that way yet. So I curtsied to him anyway, because the more you curtsy to people, the more they'll do for you, so it's worth the wear on your knees.

"Will you be riding with Sir Charles later today, my lady?" he asked me.

I'd completely forgotten about it. Hell's teeth! (It's a good thing Mrs. Champernowne can't see how much swearing I do in my head.) I don't really like horses much, but Sir Charles is one of my suitors and he's quite fun, even though he is old and plump and puffs a bit. Really he is happiest when he is at home on his country estates. He never feels very comfortable at Court, but he has been staying here to teach me to ride better—the Queen doesn't want me falling off again the next time we go hunting. And he's a good teacher. He never shouts and he explains things as often as I need, and the horses really like him. But as a husband—Lord preserve me! (That's not swearing, I checked.)

"Later," I said, and swept past with the dogs towing me excitedly.

The Orchard isn't nearly as tidy and formal as the Privy Garden. There are apple and pear and cherry trees—some of them quite climbable if I hitch up my kirtle over my belt—and redcurrant bushes and raspberries and brambles and some herbs that escaped from the kitchen gardens. Most of the time you can't be seen from the palace.

Well, the Queen can see from her bedchamber window, if she's standing in the right place. She saw me playing in the Orchard once, sword-fighting with a raspberry cane, which amused her. She has ordered that the gate be kept locked except to me, mainly to keep the older Maids of Honour and their gentlemen out of it—because they are empty-headed nitwits who are liable to ruin their whole lives for a pretty locket and some bad verse. Or that's what the Queen says.

Once I am out of sight, I often go to see a particular cherry tree that reminds me of my mother. In spring it has blossom the exact same colour as a silken gown she wore in summer. My mother died only a year ago, saving the Queen's life, and she wasn't like some of the other girls' mothers—all angry and fierce and strict. She was lovely.

The tree has tiny buds but nothing more yet. I let the dogs off the leash and they went scampering off on their short hairy legs, barking wildly. I knew why, because I could see little drifts of smoke coming from behind the compost heaps right at the end of the Orchard, near the river. The dogs yipped excitedly and disappeared behind the nearest heap. Henri came back out with a bright red shiny juggling ball, glittering with glass chips.

I grinned as I heard Masou's singsong voice saying, "Unclean beast! Get away from those. Come back, spawn of Shaitan!" Masou is my good friend, and the best boy acrobat in the Queen's Court—or so he says.

I took the ball from Henri's dribbling muzzle and went round to the hide I had made with Masou and

Ellie, my other good friend. She is a laundrymaid. We have furnished the hide to look like just another compost heap.

I have to be careful nobody finds out about our friendship or they would get into even worse trouble than me—and probably they would get beaten with birch twigs for not knowing their proper places. I hate it when they have to bow and curtsy to me in public, and call me "my lady" and "mistress." And it's very difficult not to laugh when Masou winks at me. Behind the compost heaps we can be just Ellie and Masou and Grace and nobody has to curtsy or bow to anybody.

(I had decided to write this secret information with Seville orange juice so it could only be read if the page is warmed. But when I visited the kitchen, I found that Cook has already used all the oranges for marmelada. Fie! I shall just have to be careful to keep my daybooke from prying eyes.)

Masou had lit a little fire just outside the hide, which is a dangerous thing to do, except that compost heaps do smoulder sometimes when they get too hot. He was cooking some crayfish out of the river, spitted on twigs, and Ellie was sitting over the fire warming her poor chapped hands. She works in the Whitehall laundry and, as she's an orphan, she sleeps there, too, in one of the storerooms, and she never ever has enough to eat. I feel guilty that she has to work so hard. I wanted her to be my tiring woman to take care of my gowns, but my guardian, Lord Worthy, who is one of the Queen's most trusted Privy Councillors and in charge of looking after my estates, said it was an unnecessary expense. *I* think he just wanted it to be a girl of his own choosing—so I share Fran with the other girls.

Masou was juggling absent-mindedly with his glittering red and yellow balls. When I threw him the third, he just caught it and mixed it in with the others, along with a knife and a cup and a horn spoon. I really like Masou. He's a little shorter than me, though we think he's about the same age. He comes from the south, where they're burned by the sun, and his skin is a lovely colour like a wooden casket. As he's a tumbler for the Queen's Troupe, he wears a brilliantly coloured tunic made of dozens of different brocades and velvets. He has two: a new one for performing and an old one for the rest of the time.

The dogs came scampering up, barking. Ellie scooped up Eric to give him a cuddle and then tried to rub the paw marks off her apron. I felt in the pocket of my petticoat for the couple of manchet rolls and sweetmeats I'd saved for her.

Masou sprinkled pepper on the crayfish and he and Ellie started stripping off all the legs and chewing on the bodies. I don't like crayfish—I've never even tasted them, but the look of all those legs puts me off.

"What will you perform at the St. Valentine's Ball?" I asked Masou.

He winked and made a throat-slitting movement with his finger. "Can't say," he said. "Hanged, drawn, and quartered for telling you."

I know that the Queen has devised a riddle for me to solve at the ball. I have some reputation at Court for fathoming riddles, puzzles, and the like. I am very curious (and not a little nervous!) about this one, so I thought I would see if Masou had heard anything of it—the Queen's Troupe is often privy to the Court gossip, especially if the Queen has planned a special entertainment.

"The Queen said she's got a little riddle for me—do you know what it is?" I ventured.

Masou put his hands on his chest and looked wide-eyed and innocent. "Me? Why would a poor tumbler know?"

"Lord Robert's had a bath specially," said Ellie thoughtfully. "He went down to the stews yesterday to get ready for it."

I laughed at this. Lord Robert Radcliffe of Worcester is another of the three suitors the Queen has chosen for me. He must be anxious to look—and smell—his best.

"His heart burns with passion for the beauteous Lady Grace and so he must quench it!" Masou said dramatically, so I had to kick some earth at him for making fun of me.

"Well, I think it was gentlemanly of him," said Ellie. "Very considerate. He can't afford new clothes at the moment—all the moneylenders are after him. Sir Gerald Worthy's arrived, too, and he's got a new shirt *and* a new velvet suit for the dance."

Sir Gerald Worthy is my Lord Worthy's nephew and my third suitor. I have hardly ever seen him because he has been travelling round Europe. Lord Worthy doesn't have any children and his wife died young. Sir Gerald is his only heir, which is one reason why he would be such a good match for me. I've heard he is quite handsome and that is all. I was just going to ask what else Ellie had heard about him, when I heard someone shouting my name at the Orchard gate.

I jumped up, and the dogs all started barking madly, just like we've taught them. Masou scuffed earth over the fire, Ellie gulped down the last two crayfish legs whole, and the two hid in the little compost-heap house, while I ran up through the trees.

Sure enough, Sir Charles Amesbury was standing there, big round face all red. "Come along, my lady," he said, patting his stomach. "Remember how important it is to ride every day so you become used to it." He smiled fondly. "At least you remembered to wear your riding kirtle, Lady Greensleeves."

Yes, but please, please don't sing it, I thought.

"*Alas, my love, you do me wrong,*" carolled Sir Charles as we went through the Privy Garden and down the passageways leading to the Tilting Yard. "*To cast me off discourteously, When I have loved you so long . . .*"

In fact Sir Charles has a very nice deep voice— very tuneful. He often sings for the Queen with other Court gentlemen. It's just embarrassing being sung at by a man who's old enough to be your father but wants to marry you—especially when it's such an old-fashioned song. Doesn't he know any Italian madrigals?

Two horses were saddled and waiting in the yard. I

took the dogs on their leash over to the groom. Henri started growling and snapping at Doucette's hooves, which just shows you how stupid lapdogs can be.

Sir Charles caught the horse's bridle just as she started tossing her head. "Now then," he said. "Now then, Doucette, you could squash that little dog with one foot. He's quite beneath your dignity. Gently now. See, my lady? See? With horses you move slowly and gently and so . . ."

I moved slowly and gently to pat Doucette's neck. Then Sir Charles cupped his hands for me to mount, and I managed to get myself hooked over the side-saddle without going right over the other side and falling flat on my face as I often do.

Once I had my front foot arranged, the other one firmly in the stirrup, and my whip, Sir Charles climbed up, puffing, onto the other horse. Then, suddenly, he was a completely different creature—straight and relaxed and quite at home. I'm sure that's how he looked when the Boy King was alive and Sir Charles was known for his prowess at the Tilt.

"*Greensleeves was all my joy, Greensleeves was my delight, Greensleeves was my heart of gold . . . ,*" he sang as we trotted off, and I tried not to tense up and bounce, but just to rock my bum into the saddle with the horse's movement.

While we trotted the horses to warm them up, Sir Charles talked to me. He does it so I won't think about falling off so much. Today he told me something quite sad: his twin brother died recently fighting the religious wars in France.

"I had the letter last night," he said, looking sombre. "Just the bare news of it. Alas, Hector and I were not good friends when he left and I would it had not been so. In truth, he was always the black sheep of the family—and oftentimes up to no good—but he was my brother still."

"I am sorry. Was he fighting for the Protestants?" I asked gently.

"Ay, against the foul Papist Guises," he replied grimly.

I frowned at the name of Guise. I hate them, too, and I have good reason: my mother died in one of their wicked plots to kill our Protestant Queen and put a Catholic monarch in her place.

Sir Charles distracted me then by telling me the proper way to ask a horse to canter. We practised and then tried it and dear Doucette went from a trot to the slowest canter, which was just like a hobby-horse and not frightening at all. In fact, it was almost fun to go cantering down one side of the Tilting Yard, round the fence, and then up the other side. It's the first time I've managed a canter without falling off! I was so proud!

Sir Charles laughed at my flushed face. "... *And who but my Lady Greensleeves,*" he sang, and gave me a kiss on the forehead as he helped me down. "Well done, that was very good, my lady. We'll have you out-riding the Queen yet."

"Better not let her hear you say that," I told him, and couldn't help smiling as he pretended to be dismayed.

"Oh, you wouldn't tell her, surely?" he said. "Please don't. I beg you. Shall I kneel down and beg you that way?"

I tried not to laugh. "I don't want you to hurt your poor knees," I said.

He looked cunning. "Good thought, my lady, and I must keep my hose decent for tomorrow. Are you looking forward to it?"

"No," I said, because I'm too lazy to tell polite lies. "I am not sure I am ready to choose a husband and married life."

"Small blame to you," Sir Charles sighed. "But not all ladies can be like the Queen, you know. If only you would marry me—darling Grace, Lady Cavendish—I should treat you no differently than I do now, until you were grown to your proper womanhood."

I sighed. I do like Sir Charles, but even though he's one of the three suitors the Queen has chosen for me, I don't want to marry him.

———

I just had to go and get some more ink. When I started I didn't realize how much there is to say about even a dull day.

The next thing that happened as soon as I got back from my riding lesson was a gentleman telling me the Queen was already in her chamber and I was bid attend on her. So I had to run upstairs and change into my damask again and then run to wait on the Queen.

I got there and curtsied. One of the Wardrobe tailors was kneeling in front of the Queen, sweating.

"But wherefore is Lady Grace's kirtle still not finished, Mr. Beasley?" the Queen asked disapprovingly. "Surely this is not your wonted service to me. Why so long a-making? I had desired to see it before she wears it."

"But Your Majesty," the tailor said desperately,

"the beauteous Lady Grace keeps on growing, but the cloth does not!"

I could see the Queen wanted to laugh at that, but she only told him he had her permission to burn ten more wax candles, to save his men's eyes while they sewed another hem tonight, and sent him off.

The Queen is very grand and frightening. She has red hair and snapping dark eyes and a lovely pale complexion, apart from a very few, very tiny smallpox scars, from when she was so sick while I was a little girl. She's about middling size for a woman—though she seems much taller, especially when she is displeased! And she wears the most glorious gowns imaginable, all made for her by the men of the Privy Wardrobe. She's very clever and it pleases her that I am quick enough to learn to read and write and so on. She says that she is bored by girls who can only think of jewellery and clothes. She likes me especially because she's known me all my life and my mother saved her life a year ago.

"What have you been doing to make your cheeks so red, Lady Grace?" the Queen questioned.

"I managed to canter on Doucette, Your Majesty," I told her excitedly. "And I didn't fall off once!"

She clapped her hands. "You must be tired then,"

she said. "You shall have a little light supper and go straight to your bed, for tomorrow will be a long day."

I didn't really want to be alone but there's no point arguing, so I had my light supper of pheasant pasties and salt-fish fritters, with a couple of sausages and manchet bread and some overcooked potherbs, and went to our bedchamber.

And here I am at last, in my shift and three candles lit. I'll just say my prayers and

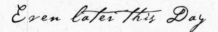

Even later this Day

I had to stop because there was a tap at the door. Ellie and Masou crept in, looking very furtive.

"You shouldn't be here, you'll get in terrible trouble," I told them.

"Fie!" said Ellie. "Look, mistress, I'm delivering your nice new smock for tomorrow, isn't it lovely?"

"Rude!" said Masou. "It's very rude to say smock. She should say shift. Isn't she rude, my lady?" He was wagging his finger at Ellie.

"Yes, and don't call me 'mistress,' or 'my lady,'" I growled.

Ellie stuck her tongue out.

"All right, let's see it," I said eagerly.

It was a beautiful smock, in fine linen, embroidered with blackwork. I recognized what Mrs. Champernowne and the Queen had been working on all autumn and smiled, feeling quite touched. The Queen was as excited about the St. Valentine's Ball as if I were her own true daughter.

"We just ironed it. Look at all them ruffles—I did 'em myself," said Ellie, who was learning to be a proper laundrywoman. She folded it neatly and put it in my clothes chest.

Masou came over and sat on the bed. He had a little tiny pot made of alabaster. "See, this is kohl," he said, opening it. "If you put a little, just a very little, around your eyes, they will look beautiful and sparkling."

"I don't like wearing face paint," I said, and pushed the pot away.

He laughed at me. "Not white lead and cinnabar, no, but this will be as if your eyes had grown that way."

"Masou, please, please tell what the Queen is planning for me," I begged. "She won't breathe a word."

He put his finger on his lips and winked. "Mr. Somers himself said we must not tell, and when he said it he was staring straight at me," he whispered.

I sighed. Masou would not cross the leader of the Queen's Troupe.

Then he and Ellie did a ridiculous little dance, while juggling some of Lady Sarah's dozens of face-paint pots. Finally, they replaced the pots, oh, so carefully, and backed out of the door into the passage, where they immediately became serious and well behaved. They do make me laugh.

I hate not knowing what Her Majesty is up to, even though I know she would never be cruel to me as she sometimes is to other courtiers. Oh, Lord, preserve me. I hope I don't have to dance by myself! Or sing!

Now I must sleep.

I should not really be writing this at all. We're in the Queen's Chapel and the Palace Chaplain has been preaching for at least four hours. Maybe not quite that long, but I'm sure it is nearly dinner time. I am pretending to take notes on his sermon (hah!).

When we processed to chapel this morning, we passed by the Great Hall. It seemed all the Household were there, hanging up red silk banners and scurrying to and fro to fetch ladders and hang tinsel hearts for the ball. When I saw the hustle and bustle, I wasn't sure if I was excited or terrified, and my heart beat fast.

The Queen isn't listening to the sermon, either. She's snorting quietly at something in the paper she's reading. She always brings her red boxes with her so she can read during the service—as she told me, it's necessary for her to be there, but the good

Lord knows how busy she is with the idiots of her Council, and will forgive her if she uses the time productively. I'm sure that's right.

I have to stop now. The Chapel Boys are singing— so beautiful, like birds. I must pack my ink away— the service will finish soon.

Later this Day

I am sitting in a window seat with my daybooke and penner and I shouldn't be doing this AT ALL. I am all dressed now in my rose-velvet gown, ready for the ball, and if I got ink on my gown . . . But I feel so scared, my heart is thudding and my palms are like slugs. I have to do something. It's the sleeves I'm worried about: they're white, so any speck of ink will show. I suppose I could get Fran to unlace them and put another pair on, but I don't know which of my pairs of sleeves would match.

After Chapel I had a little food I wasn't hungry for, and then Mrs. Champernowne called me to the Queen's Withdrawing Chamber, where all the closets are, to help me dress. First, I had a bath in the Queen's own tub with rose-water soap from Castile and then, when I was dry, I put on my new smock.

I expect Lady Sarah and Mary Shelton were flurrying around in our chamber, arguing over partlets and false fronts and making accusations about pots of perfume. But it was peaceful in the Queen's Withdrawing Chamber so I had plenty of time to get nervous.

We waited behind a screen while the tub was taken out by some of the Queen's Serving Men, and then Mrs. Champernowne rubbed her hands to make them warm. "Now then," she said to me. "Please do not wriggle, Lady Grace."

When Ellie gets dressed she laces her bodice over her smock, puts on a petticoat and her kirtle, slips her cap, shoes, and wooden pattens on, and there she is.

Well, me getting ready for a feast takes an awful lot longer than that. Mrs. Champernowne brushed my hair, and her own tiring woman brought my new partlet, all covered with embroidered flowers. The linen is transparently fine; I was scared I'd tear it when I put my head through the neck hole. And I hate the feeling of having the tabs tied under my armpits. It tickles! The Queen has given me a new pair of white silk stockings with rose-wool garters and new rose-embroidered dancing slippers. The staymaker had brought my new stays. They're cut French-style, and they're so tight round the waist I can hardly breathe. Even my bumroll is new, though my petticoat and farthingale are altered ones of my mother's. The top petticoat is of white damask, embroidered with roses.

My gown is just *amazing*! It is very heavy, because it's mostly made of rose velvet and all in a piece—so I had to sort of dive in and slide. I popped out with my hair everywhere and my arms waving. It took ages for Mrs. Champernowne and Fran to do all the lacing and tying together. The silver aiglets on the ends of the laces were decorated with roses so I knew they were my mother's. Suddenly my chest felt stuffed full with sadness that she wasn't there to help me dress for my first proper grown-up feast.

"Oh, sweetheart," said Mrs. Champernowne. She gave my shoulders a squeeze, then dabbed my eyes and nose for me. "If you make your nose all red, we will have to paint it with white, look you."

I nodded and tried to direct my thoughts elsewhere.

When they had finished, they turned me round to look in the Queen's own looking glass, which is huge and made of Venetian glass and worth as much as a good horse! It was as if a tall lady had come in and was facing me. While Fran tied a small ruff round my neck, I curtsied to her—the reflection did the same. Well, I knew it was me, really, but I didn't believe it until then.

"There now," said Mrs. Champernowne, sounding satisfied. "A very beautiful Maid of Honour."

"Do you think so?" I thought the strange lady staring at me from the looking glass certainly looked better than I usually do.

"Any man should think himself lucky to have you to wife, my dear," she said. "Of course, *Sir Gerald* will be able to buy you as many gowns as you like."

I smiled to myself. My Lord Worthy had clearly been drumming up support for his nephew. "What about Sir Charles?" I asked, partly because I wanted to put her off the scent of my Lord Robert, who is probably my favourite.

Mrs. Champernowne sniffed. "Sir Charles would more likely give you horses," she answered. "And as for that young fool, Lord Robert, I hope you do not throw yourself away on him. Sir Gerald was putting him right on something the other day, and all Lord Robert could do was gawp at him."

It is true that Lord Robert can be a bit tongue-tied, but at least he isn't old. He is about twenty. I wonder what he was arguing about with Sir Gerald. I didn't ask because Mrs. Champernowne clearly wanted me to. And I don't want any more good advice about how nice Sir Gerald is.

"Off with you now," Mrs. Champernowne said. "And do not so much as speckle your kirtle, Lady Grace, or I will birch you, by God, Queen or no Queen. Her Majesty must dress now."

I slipped my pattens on to protect my slippers and wobbled through the door. As soon as I got into the passage, I found Ellie and Masou peeking round the corner from the back stairs.

Ellie clapped her hands. "You look beautiful, my lady," she said wistfully. "Truly beautiful."

"Oh, fie," I replied. "Anyone could look beautiful in this dress."

Ellie shook her head. She has a bump on the bridge of her nose and quite a lot of spots and her hands are red from the washing soap.

"Anyway, it's very uncomfortable," I added. "It's too tight round my waist and I can't bend my arms properly and my neck's stiff from the ruff and I dare neither breathe nor scratch!"

Masou made an elaborate bow to me, then came

close with his little pot of kohl and dabbed a tiny amount on my eyelids. It tickled and I was scared he'd get my ruff dirty, but Masou is very quick and dextrous. I looked in the side of a polished silver jug which stands on a chest near the window, and it did make my eyes look more . . . mysterious, I suppose. Masou was wearing some for his stage paint already. "You have no necklace," he pointed out.

He was right, I didn't.

"Why would that be?" He bowed again, smiling, and I knew it was the clue to the Queen's riddle that I'd asked for. Then he was off with Ellie because they both had lots to do before the ball.

Very late, this same Day

I am writing this by the watch candle. I'm in my own bedchamber at last. In the other bed, Lady Sarah and Mary Shelton are asleep. Lady Sarah is snoring like a pig, while Mary Shelton is snoring like a badger.

I had to stop quickly earlier and hide everything away because Mrs. Champernowne was coming. (I got Ellie to come and fetch my daybooke and penner to the bedchamber later on.)

Everything in my head is all muddled up—there is so much to tell of this night's events!

Mrs. Champernowne fetched me to the Presence Chamber and I sat there on a cushion with the other Maids of Honour, feeling like a wooden doll and wishing I could run round the Privy Garden half a dozen times. I didn't. I think Mrs. Champernowne really would have birched me, if I'd done that. But I did wriggle a bit because of a fleabite on my back.

"Now stay still, Lady Grace," Mrs. Champernowne scolded. "Remember, the stuff for that gown cost Her Majesty hundreds of pounds, never mind the tailoring!"

I goggled at her.

"You could buy a house in the City of Westminster with that, look you. So none of your hoydenish tricks," she went on.

I was really glad she hadn't spotted me using pen and ink.

After a long while of waiting and talking quietly, it was time to go. I felt sick with nerves. The Queen arrived in her wonderful gown of cloth of silver and black velvet. Everybody else was in white or silver damask to match her—it's quite an honour that I was allowed to wear rose. Lady Bedford, the most favoured Lady-in-Waiting, arranged the Queen's long black damask train and veil and then we all set off, walking two by two down the passages where the Gentlemen of the Guard stood in their red velvet, and all the other courtiers cheered and clapped. I had to walk with Lady Sarah, who was furious about all the special treatment I'd received and wouldn't talk to me.

The Great Hall was festooned with red and purple ribbons and tinsel hearts dangling from the beams. The Maids of Honour don't often go in there because the Queen likes to eat in the Privy Parlour and we usually keep her company. (Last month, the Queen was so busy with paperwork and Council meetings that she had her food brought on a tray, and we had to find our food as best we could. In the end, I gave Ellie some money and sent her out to get pasties for all of us at the nearest cookshop. We all burned our mouths because they were still so hot!)

We lined up behind the top table on the dais, facing all the other tables in the hall. The Queen made some sort of speech of welcome, but I was still feeling sick so I didn't listen. I looked quickly for my suitors, but they were all at the other end of the top table, next to Lord Worthy, ignoring each other. The Queen had kindly arranged things so that they wouldn't be staring at me. I saw Ellie right down the other end of the hall and she waved to me, only I couldn't wave back because of being dignified.

I thought I would run lunatic with all the to-ing and fro-ing. I hate feasting. I hate having to sit around being polite and conversing while my stomach's rumbling like a cart on cobbles as we wait for ages for the food to arrive. This time there was a *really* long wait while the serving men, squires, and pageboys sorted themselves out by the hatch outside. Then I nearly jumped out of my skin when the musicians blared on the trumpets to announce them. They processed in to very loud stately music, carrying beef and venison and swan and suckling pig and some chickens—and a game pie as big as a wellhead. I felt quite sorry for them, having to carry the food above their heads on huge silver platters. Then there was *another* long wait while they took the meat to the carving table for carving.

By this time, my mouth was so dry and my stomach so clenched up about the dancing (and whatever the Queen was going to do), I couldn't eat anything at all except a bit of manchet bread and butter and a few candied carrots and potherbs, like the ones decorating the sallet. So it was wasted.

The only good thing that happened was that when

the serving man brought me the candied carrots, he had a very strained expression on his face. Then, when he leaned over to get the plate of fried-bread sippets, he farted very loudly—which made me and Mary Shelton giggle.

And as for swan-meat—ptui! (Mrs. Champernowne says a lady must only spit discreetly into her handkerchief, but I can spit in writing, if I want.) They only have it because it looks so pretty. It's all put back together after carving and covered with a suit of swan's feathers with a cunningly carved head and neck as well, so it looks as if it's still alive and swimming on the silver platter. But I don't care if it is a royal bird, it tastes fishy and horrible—even worse than turkey!

Lady Sarah would not talk to me at all during the two covers of food; she just kept chatting to Mary Shelton and Carmina, who was next to Mary. It was fine—at least I didn't have to try to chat back with my mouth so dry. Mrs. Champernowne told the page to give me watered wine, which helped a bit. I had to sip it really carefully, though, because I was terrified of spilling any on my gown.

After the first set of dishes, there was a pause. I was just beginning to relax, thanks to the wine, when *bam-bam-da-da-bam-bam!* I nearly fell off the bench with fright.

In came French Louis with a big drum, banging on it like a madman. Behind him were the dwarf twins, Peter and Paul, juggling with red satin hearts, and behind them was Mr. Will Somers, the Queen's Fool, flipping slowly over and over and jumping up to turn over in the air. And then, with the drum going *bam-da-da-bam-da-da-bam* and the trumpets making an even more awful noise than they did to start with, in came Little John, the huge strongman, holding a pole on his head. And at the top of the pole, standing on a little platform about the size of your two hands, was Masou. I stared with my mouth open. I was already tense! I thought this was really too much. Out of the corner of my eye I saw Ellie watching, too, white as a sheet, hands to her mouth.

And as if that weren't dangerous enough, Masou stood on one leg and started juggling with batons. He saw us, grinned, and winked at me. And then he tilted, waved his arms, wobbled, and fell . . .

I couldn't help it—I screamed. Everybody else was screaming, too. But then, in midair, Masou turned a backwards somersault and landed perfectly on his feet like a cat. And then he caught the batons he'd been juggling and carried on—while doing a jig. Everybody whooped and clapped; even the Queen was laughing and clapping.

I clapped, too, but only a bit because my hands were shaking so much. Ellie looked as if she'd nearly fainted. I don't know what gets into Masou when he tumbles for an audience. I think he goes wood-wild in the head.

The Queen spoke to one of the pages and Mr. Somers brought Masou up to the dais to be presented to the Queen. I didn't hear what she said, but when all the tumblers bounced and jumped and cartwheeled off again, Masou turned somersaults in the air and his face was shining.

And then it was time for the banquet course and we all stood up and processed out to the Banqueting House in the garden. They had taken it out of storage and put it up specially, and the rude pictures on the canvas walls of Venus and Cupid had lasted quite well—the paint had hardly cracked and Venus's naked bottom was still quite pink.

I like the banqueting course usually, with all the jellies and sweetmeats and custards—and the beautiful marchpane subtlety in the middle. This one was a sculpture of Venus again, with Cupid aiming an arrow made of liquorice, all made in pink sugar plate and really pretty. Except I could see that there were three blue velvet cushions lying on the table in front of the banquet, and little squares of white silk covered the things that were resting on them.

So that meant I couldn't even enjoy the sweetmeats—like the marmelada of quinces, which is my favourite, or the vanilla egg creams. I was too busy trying not to stare at those cushions. On one was a sort of roundish lump, on the second was a long and pointed shape, and the thing on the third one just looked like a heap of peas!

They had laid a floor of polished wood to dance on and the musicians in the corner began a Burgermeister dance to break the ice. It's such a silly German dance; you can't be dignified when you're wagging fingers and linking arms.

All the Maids of Honour swept off in a long line to face the gentlemen and bow and curtsy. Somehow, Lord Robert had managed to barge into the row facing me, so we partnered and, while I held his hand and did the first bit of dancing, he stared at me and went red and said, "Umm . . . er . . . Lady Grace . . . um . . ."

"What?" I said breathlessly. But by that time it

was his turn to hop and point his toes, and by the time he'd come back to me he'd missed his chance because we had to go back and change partners.

It was like that every time he looked at me, or we took hands in the dance: he was trying to say something he'd clearly made up beforehand, but each time he just stammered and looked sweaty. It was very irritating. I think that a lot of Lord Robert's manly silence is Lord Robert not knowing what to say. Still, at least he's only twenty. That's something. And he has quite good legs. The other girls say he has high birth and low pockets—by which I suppose they mean he has no money and his estates are mortgaged. But I don't care about that as long as he loves me. I've got plenty of money of my own. Though it would be nice if he could say something other than "Um . . ." occasionally.

Next there was a Pavane, otherwise known as the most boring dance in the world. Dances are for jumping about and getting breathless. What's the point of all that stately walking to and fro in lines, holding hands, turning, bowing, curtsying, and step-ping backwards and forwards? Yawn! For this one I got Sir Charles, who was looking unusually sour and bad-tempered.

"At least this is a tune we know," I said to him, as he walked me back and forth.

I'd realized that the musicians were playing "Greensleeves."

"Hm?" He looked puzzled. "What do you mean, my lady?"

I nudged him in the ribs. "It's 'Greensleeves,'" I said. "The song you always sing when we go riding?"

He smiled wanly. "Oh yes, how silly of me to forget. 'Greensleeves,' of course . . . *Ta dah, di dah, di dah, dah dah dah* . . ." His voice was flat.

I tutted. "You seem to have a bad throat, Sir Charles," I said. "You really should not sing. And nor should you dance."

Not that he can. A Pavane is about all he can manage, though his knees seemed a bit less stiff.

Next thing, the Master of Ceremonies announced a Volta. We've just done it in dancing class. It's very scandalous because you have to show your knees! But the Queen loves it. I myself don't like the bit where you have to dance while the gentleman stands there, or the bit when he gets to show off. What I like is when the gentleman takes hold of the lower edge of your stays and lifts you up as you jump and bang your feet together. That's great fun. Though last Tuesday morning the dancing master was very upset. "You are supposed to come down like a feather! A *feather*!" he shouted at me, when a painting fell off the wall of the Long Gallery.

As we lined up, ready to go round to our partners, I thought that Sir Gerald was going to partner Lady Sarah (whose bosom was nearly hanging out over her bodice again—honestly, I know not why Mrs. Champernowne doesn't chide her for it). But then Lord Worthy moved next to Sir Gerald and said something in his ear, and he changed places with another gentleman, who looked very pleased.

So for the Volta I got Sir Gerald. He smiled and bowed and looked straight at me. The new gentleman was staring at Lady Sarah's chest, but Sir Gerald was looking at my face. (Well, I've got nothing to see further down, even in a French-cut bodice.) He has one of those very handsome faces, all straight lines and angles, with quizzical black eyebrows. He's tall, so it looks as if he's staring down his nose at me. I've played some Primero with Sir Gerald (I won! Ha ha!) and walked in the Privy Garden for our formal meetings, but that's all. He's quite old—though not as ancient as Sir Charles. I think he had a wife, but she died in childbirth. At least he's neither fat nor tongue-tied.

"Your ladyship is more beautiful than I have ever

seen you," he said. "Rose velvet becomes you, Lady Grace."

I tried to blush, but couldn't. "Thank you, Sir Gerald," I replied.

I'd done my bit of the footwork so he did his. The thing about a Volta is, if you can dance, it gives you a chance to show off. Sir Gerald can certainly dance. I've never seen anything like it, the way he jumped and kicked and moved his feet in time to the fast drumbeats. Then it was time for me to jump and, when he caught hold of my stays and lifted me, I went higher than I ever do with the dancing master, who's always complaining that we've utterly undone his back. I went right up, twirled, and came down quite well, too, because I'd gone up so straight. He steadied me as I landed and lifted me again, so I was breathless by the time the jumping bit was over.

"Do you think Lord Robert could do that, my lady?" he whispered, and he wasn't even breathing hard as we paced around in a circle with others of our set. "Or Sir Charles?"

I know Sir Charles couldn't—he makes heavy weather out of helping me into the saddle. But Lord Robert? He's young and quite skinny but I think he's strong, too. I saw him tossing Mary Shelton into the air without much difficulty. And she's no slender reed.

"Don't throw yourself away on rustics," Sir Gerald went on as we joined up once more. "Lord Robert is poor and Sir Charles will always love horses more than you. Marry me."

And then the dance parted us, leaving me rather annoyed. I really don't like being told what to think. Besides, I knew who I liked more and it certainly wasn't Sir Very-very-sure-of-himself Gerald. Let Lady Sarah have him.

At last the Queen clapped her hands, the dancing music stopped, and she beckoned me forward. "Good friends," she said, while the musicians in the corner played a pretty, soft tune on their viols. "Today is a joyous day for our dear Lady Grace. She has petitioned me to marry her to some gentleman of my choosing . . ."

I hadn't, but I know that's what my father put in his will before he died serving the Queen in France in the first years of her reign.

". . . and I have chosen three goodly nobles, each of whom would be a fine husband for any woman. But which man will kindle our Lady Grace's young heart?"

There was a murmur and then Lord Robert came

forward and dropped to one knee. "Umm . . . I will, Y-your Majesty," he stammered.

Behind him came Sir Gerald, who also kneeled. "Your Gracious Majesty . . . who by offering Lady Grace increases her own grace . . . ," he began. I saw Lord Worthy smile fondly at his nephew's charm. "My Lady Grace needs a *man* to her bridal bed, not a mouse. *I* am the most manly of the suitors," Sir Gerald declared.

At this, the other Maids of Honour giggled a little, and Lord Robert went purply red and looked at the polished floor.

Sir Charles then came forward and put his knee down firmly. "But *I* will be the best husband for Lady Grace, Your Majesty," he said. "Because she and I have friendship in our favour."

I looked at Sir Charles, feeling very uncomfortable. Yes, we were friends—of sorts—but he did look particularly old tonight. And his face looked not nearly as pink and jolly as usual. Perhaps he was nervous, too.

The Queen clapped her hands and smiled. "You offer yourselves, but what of your inmost hearts?" she said. "And what of Grace's young and unschooled heart? We shall try if heart can speak to heart upon this Feast of St. Valentine." She turned to me and beckoned, so I went forward and curtsied to one knee.

She caught my hand and raised me up. "Each of Lady Grace's lovers has presented a gift, unmarked and unknown. Now it is for Lady Grace to select the gift that likes her heart best, and so, the man who will have her heart."

My heart went *thump! lurch!* and I wanted to be sick, which I obviously couldn't, standing next to the Queen like that.

"Come, my dear, make appraisal of the gifts," the Queen commanded.

I went and looked at the cushions, pulling the white silk squares off each gift. One was a small, silver-chased ivory flask with a lid that took off and became a cup—the sort of thing the Queen carries in her sleeve when she hunts, with aqua vitae in it.

The second was a small jewelled knife, set with garnets and pearls, with a pearl Cupid on the end—very pretty. Of course, I have an eating knife, but it just has a bone hilt and a plain leather scabbard, so it isn't pretty enough to wear on special occasions. I liked the knife—I picked it up and drew it to see whether it was just for show. There was a sharp steel blade, so I put it back carefully.

The third cushion bore a pearl necklace with gold

links—quite simple, but very long, so you could wrap it round your neck and have it dangle all the way to your waist, or wear it as a snood round your hair. I touched the pearls. I am very fond of pearls; my mother used to wear them. I always wear a little pearl ring that she gave me. And what was it Masou had said? I glanced across at him, playing a lute in the corner with the musicians. Why wasn't I wearing a necklace? Good question.

Then I stepped back and curtsied to the Queen. "May I explain what I judge from these gifts, Your Majesty?" I asked, and tried to think of something clever to say. "This flask, Your Majesty, is beautifully made for bringing spirits to revive one's spirits when hunting. Perhaps Sir Charles, who has been helping my poor horsemanship, is hoping I will need it soon. From this, I guess a great ability to love, a heart deep enough for anyone to drain, a generous and kindly nature."

Sir Charles bowed.

"But I fear it will be a long time before I can ride well enough to keep up with the Queen's Hunt," I concluded.

I turned to the long necklace of pearls with the gold links. "Here is a rope of pearls. He who gave it knows my favourite jewel is the pearl and has given a long enough length that I will not feel constricted by it. I read sensitivity to my likes in the giver. But, nonetheless, is the rope of pearls meant to bind me tight, my Lord Robert?"

As usual, Lord Robert reddened and bowed. Sir Gerald was looking very smug now.

"And the beautiful dagger. Surely it speaks of a keen intelligence and a cutting wit. I was tempted because I would like so pretty a knife—but who woos with a blade? Surely a knife cuts the knot and does not tie it, Sir Gerald?"

Now Sir Gerald was scowling. It gave an ugly sneer to his mouth. He knocked back another silver cup of wine and held it out for a pageboy to refill.

I turned to the Queen and went down on one knee again. "In conclusion, Your Majesty, I am happy in your service. I yet have no desire to marry."

The Queen shook her head, smiling sadly. "It was my promise to your parents, Grace," she said. "You must have a husband to look after your estates."

"Well, in that case . . ." I stood, sighed, trailed my fingers along the dagger and the flask, and then picked up the lovely pearl necklace and looped it carefully round my neck. "I choose my Lord Robert's gift."

He looked absolutely moonstruck. Quite like a calf with the bellyache, as Masou described him. I had to squash the urge to laugh.

He came forward with his face as red as ever to kiss my hand. "Um . . . Lady Grace . . . I, um . . . Um," he said.

The musicians struck up another dance tune as Sir Gerald rolled his eyes and drank another cup of aqua vitae. Lord Worthy hurried over and whispered in his ear again, which provoked a snarl.

Lord Robert and I danced a passage of the Volta, which got everyone staring, but that's what the musicians were playing. And yes, when Lord Robert lifted me, he felt strong enough and he steadied me when I landed—but he still didn't manage to say anything except "Um" and "Er." I felt quite sorry for him, though at least when I'm married to him *I* shall be able to talk as much as I like.

The other courtiers joined in and other couples went jigging and jumping and whizzing past us. I saw Sir Charles sitting at the side near a bank of candles, watching us rather sourly. Then Sir Gerald came through with a rather stout Lady-in-Waiting, and barged Lord Robert out of the way and trod on his foot. Off he went again.

Nobody else had noticed, but Lord Robert was gripping his sword. "I h-hate him," he sputtered.

I put my hand on his, gripping his sword hilt. "But you won and he lost," I said. "Why not be kind and forgiving?"

"My Lady Grace . . . ," said Lord Robert, "you . . . are . . . so . . . w-wonderful."

Well, it was the longest speech he has ever made me, and it was quite flattering, so I smiled and kissed his cheek.

Dancing makes me thirsty and so, when the music stopped, I fanned myself and asked for something to drink. Lord Robert went to the sideboard where the pages and serving men were pouring wine. He waited patiently for Lord Worthy to get himself some mead, turning to survey the hall before taking a goblet for himself and a little Venetian glass cup of a flower water for me.

Sir Charles and Sir Gerald were collecting the gifts I had turned down. I was sorry I had offended Sir Charles, because usually he really is a nice old thing. Sir Gerald looked furious—pale, eyes glittering, with little patches of colour on his cheeks. He rocked as he swept up the dagger and stuck it in his belt. "Only a silly little chit of a girl chooses a stripling boy over a man grown," he snarled. "Does she think Lord Robert will look after her? She'll be wiping his bum for him."

He glugged back his wine, not noticing some pink spots on his ruff. He held it out to be refilled, but the pages and serving men are given strict orders by the Queen that anyone who looks drunk is not to be served. She won't have scenes at her Court as they do at the King of Scotland's, for instance.

"Oh, for Christ's sake, have we run out of booze already?" Sir Gerald demanded vulgarly.

I took my flower water out of Lord Robert's hand because he was scowling at Sir Gerald, and turning pink at being called a boy. I was very glad I hadn't chosen the dagger now; who wants to be married to a bully?

Then the crowd parted, and there stood the Queen. Those who knew Her Majesty well could see that, inside, she was furious. "If you need wine to drown your sorrows, Sir Gerald, I am sure that the winner of Lady Grace's heart will be magnanimous enough to offer his own," she said lightly.

Lord Robert went a darker red and his fingers clenched on the goblet in his hand.

Lord Worthy hurried forward and took Sir

Gerald's arm. "No need, no need," he said comfortably. "Come, nephew, I think you've had enough already."

"If Sir Gerald is in need of wine, then wine he must have," declared the Queen, in the tone that nobody likes to hear. "Perhaps you won't accept it from your victor, Sir Gerald . . . ," she added, as she glided across the floor and held out her hand for Lord Robert's cup.

I stood on Lord Robert's toe and he bowed jerkily and handed his goblet to the Queen.

"But surely you will accept it from me," she finished.

As she glided back I realized Her Majesty was being very clever, smoothing over the quarrel, perhaps preventing a duel. She handed Lord Robert's cup of wine to Sir Gerald and of course he had to bow to her and then he really did have to drink it.

"From so fair and merciful a hand, what can I do but accept?" he asked, and drank it all down in one go. Then he made to bow again, lost his balance, and fell flat on his nose!

I laughed and the Queen laughed, and so did everybody else, especially Lord Robert. Only Lord Worthy was still upset. He rushed over, pulled Sir Gerald to his feet, and hissed something in his ear.

Sir Gerald bowed again, this time less unsteadily. "Your Majesty, by your leave, I think I had best get to bed," he mumbled.

"Yes," said the Queen pointedly. "I think that would be wise, Sir Gerald. The oblivion of the wine cup is no real cure for a broken heart, but at least there can be the oblivion of sleep, and all shall be forgotten in the morning."

I thought she was being very nice to him; she is normally much sharper with anyone who drinks enough to fall over. Though I was very surprised that Sir Gerald was upset enough at my rejecting him to get so drunk.

"Thank you, Your Majesty," he said.

Lord Worthy went with him to the door, but the Queen summoned him back. "Come, my old friend, my Lord Worthy," she called. "As long as my lord the Earl of Leicester is away, I need a partner. Come dance with me."

He could hardly refuse, but he didn't look very happy about it as he took the Queen's hand, bowed, kissed it, and then led off with her in the French Farandol.

After all that, I was feeling so hot in my rose-velvet gown that I decided if I didn't cool off, I'd melt. So I slipped my pattens on and went out of the

Banqueting House into the Privy Garden, where it was quite cool and dank. I passed several bushes rather full of people, two by two, and one with a young gentleman flat on his back singing to the stars. I walked quickly on past the maze, to the part that gives onto the kitchens and the buttery.

Ellie was there with someone I recognized as Pip, Sir Gerald's manservant, who was flapping his hands about.

"I only wanted to brush it out," he was saying. "Just shake it and brush it and perhaps dust it with rose-leaf powder before hanging it, so it would be fit for the Court another day. But he was in a rage, you know, quite beside himself. . . ."

Ellie tutted and popped into one of the store sheds to emerge with a bucket. "Where did you say he was sick?"

"On the edge of the mat," Pip told her. "I'm sorry, I would do it myself, but . . ."

"Not to worry." Ellie made a wry face. "I'm used to it after feasts."

She caught sight of me and grinned, rolling her eyes. Her sleeves were rolled up and she had her apron on.

". . . so I'm sure the canions will be crumpled and his ruff bent. And when he wakes up tomorrow and finds I haven't undressed him, I'll be the one to get the blame, you know. It'll all be my fault and I shouldn't wonder if he doesn't kick me out then and there and . . ."

Poor Pip was wringing his hands. I'm more pleased than ever that I turned down Sir Gerald's pretty knife—you can tell a lot from the way someone treats their servants and it's *not* a good sign that Pip is so scared of Sir Gerald.

"He's in one of my Lord Worthy's chambers, isn't he?" asked Ellie. "Why don't I knock on the door, go in, and do the floor, and if that doesn't wake him, you'll know it's safe enough to go in yourself and put everything away before you go to bed?"

Pip looked pathetically grateful. "Would you do that? Be careful, he can be violent when he's drunk and angry," he warned.

"Oh, fie!" sniffed Ellie. "If I can't dodge a kick when the kicker's blind drunk, I deserve a bruise on my bum. Don't you worry, Pip, I'll see to it." She gave me a wink and hurried past to the Grace-and-Favour Chambers, lugging the bucket of lye and a floorcloth.

I turned and went back to the Banqueting House, where the light from the banks of candles was shining out through the painted canvas, throwing silhouettes of Venus and Adonis onto the grass. So I stood and looked for a while, although I was getting chilly.

Somebody came near and turned to bow to me, then took my hand. "Who is it?" I asked.

"Robert," came the reply.

I smiled and relaxed and let him hold my hand. In the darkness I could only see the shape of him.

"When may I k-kiss your lips, my Lady Grace?"

Another long speech! Perhaps it was easier for him to talk when no one could see.

"When we're properly handfasted next month," I said primly.

He kissed my hand instead and I let him. It was very romantic and proper. "A long t-time away. W-will you d-dance again, Lady Grace?"

"With you, my lord?" I said. "Of course."

I let him lead me back to the dancing and we joined the line for another Farandol, which I thought was quite brave of Lord Robert, considering how often I had trod on his toes during the Volta.

We danced several more dances together. Sir Charles came up, still looking miserable, and offered to shake Lord Robert's hand, which I thought was quite good of him. He stared at me all the time, though, which worried me. Then I saw Pip, Sir Gerald's man, come back into the hall and speak to

Lord Worthy—who was holding the Queen's fan for her while she watched Sir Christopher Hatton, one of the Queen's favourites, demonstrate a new measure in the Volta. Lord Worthy spoke sharply to him, glancing over at Lord Robert and me once or twice. From the hand gestures, it looked as if Pip was explaining how Sir Gerald had been sick and gone to bed, and Lord Worthy looked a little less worried then.

At last the Queen decided that she had danced enough—and so, naturally, had all her Maids of Honour and Ladies-in-Waiting. We formed up in a line, a little less neat-looking than it had been on our arrival, and processed out, while the musicians played and the men started gathering together and talking about taking a boat down to Paris Garden.

When I went to help the Queen undress she waved me away. "No, my dear, take Fran to your chamber and get yourself to bed. You must be exhausted."

I suddenly noticed how sore my feet were and how my legs ached and how my stomach felt strange from being squashed together by my tight new stays, so I kneeled and kissed her hand.

"Was this St. Valentine's Feast to your liking, my dear?" She smiled at me.

"Oh yes, Your Majesty. I've had a wonderful time," I told her. And it was true—once I'd got the business of the gifts out of the way.

As I took my leave, the Queen added, "Grace, you will find something waiting on your pillow, my dear."

I curtsied again, wondering what it was, and made my way with Fran to my chamber.

Fran unlaced and unhooked me very quickly, and the rose-velvet kirtle and bodice came off. Then the petticoat and farthingale and bumroll and the other petticoat, and then, at last, Fran unlaced the stays and I said, "Ooooff!"

It's pleasing to wear stays and know how small your waist is, but it's even better to take them off and let everything sag. And then, of course, your innards start working again, so you really need to be alone, and Fran knew it, so she smiled and gave me a kiss on the cheek.

"You were beautiful this evening, Lady Grace. You outshone them all," she said.

Now I know it isn't true because no one with mousy hair can outshine Sarah Copper-locks Bartelmy, but it was nice of her to say it, so I kissed her back.

She went out, carrying my kirtle and French stays for brushing and hanging up in a closet.

I took off the pearl necklace my Lord Robert had given me and placed it beside my bed, then changed into my ordinary smock that I wear to bed and used the close-stool.

Fran had poured out some fresh rose-water so I could wash my face and I used my new toothcloth for my teeth and fennel-water to rinse out the almond-and-salt paste.

So here I am. There is a fire in the grate and it's not cold, so I have put my dressing gown on to sit in my favourite corner and write everything down.

Perhaps as I am writing all this in my daybooke, my mother will peek down from heaven and read it, too, so it's as if I am writing to her. I know she would have enjoyed me dancing at the feast. I wonder what she would have thought of my suitors? I think she would have approved of my choice. I know she wouldn't have liked Sir Gerald and I'm sure she would have understood about Sir Charles being too old.

I am finding it hard to keep my eyes open now. I must retire to bed.

The early hours

I had intended to sleep, but now cannot. I am all unsettled and must write this down, too.

When I pulled back the bedcovers I saw a small package on the pillow. At first I wondered which gentleman had placed it there, but then I remembered the Queen's words as I left her chamber. I picked it up and held it to the candle—then had to put it down again quickly as I recognized the writing on the front. It was my mother's writing, dated 14 February 1568, the night she died.

Sometimes I wish that when it happened, on that night a year ago, instead of being where I really was, tucked up fast asleep in a truckle bed in my mother's chamber, I was an angel. Then, God willing, I could have saved her.

I shall tell the story properly, as if I were a storyteller at the fair. Then perhaps I'll get through it.

I've heard that making a tale of a terrible matter may tame it, so the memory no longer rises up and fights away sleep.

My mother, Lady Margaret Cavendish, was a Gentlewoman of the Bedchamber and one of the Queen's closest friends. On 13 February 1568, after kissing me goodnight, she was sitting down to a quiet supper with the Queen, when a man came from Mr. Secretary Cecil to say there was an urgent dispatch from Scotland. The Queen told me she kissed my mother, said she would be back in ten minutes, and suggested my mother try a little wine to help her megrim headache. Then she went to hear the news from Scotland.

And my mother poured herself some wine and drank it. . . .

When I think about it, this is where I imagine being an angel. I fly into the room just as my mother takes up her goblet and I shout, "My lady, do not drink the wine!" And as I would have been a very impressive sight, what with the wings and halo and all, my mother drops the goblet on the rush matting, and then one of the Queen's canary birds—the vicious one that pecks your hair—flies down and drinks it and falls over and dies and so she knows that the wine is poisoned. And then the Queen comes back and they call the guards and test the wine and the doctor finds it contains a deadly poison called darkwort. Then everyone bolts the doors and quarters the Court and so they catch the evil Frenchman sent by the Guises to kill the Queen. . . .

But that's not what happened. My mother drank the Queen's wine and took terribly sick.

The first I knew was when Mrs. Champernowne came and woke me up and wrapped her own furry dressing gown round me. I was too sleepy to walk straight, so she gave me a piggyback—I can hardly believe she did it, when she's so sharp and cross, but she did. And then she brought me into the Queen's own bedchamber.

I could see the Queen was putting pen and ink away and she had tear tracks all down her cheeks. There was incense burning in a little dish, but you could still smell a nasty, dusty, bitter scent in the air. Mrs. Champernowne was crying, too, and I started as well, though I was still too sleepy to know why. Then I looked at the Queen's bed, and saw my mother lying there with her stays open. She had been bled, for her arm was bandaged. And I woke up properly.

My mother's eyes were shut, and her face looked

like candle wax. There was a kind of yellow froth at the corners of her mouth.

I rushed to her. "Is it plague?" I whispered.

"No, Grace," the Queen replied gravely. "If only it were, for she might recover. I think she has taken poison meant for me. The doctor has gone to look at the vomitus."

The door opened and my uncle, Dr. Cavendish, hurried in, wrapped in a fur-lined gown. He came to the other side of the Queen's bed, took my mother's pulses again, felt her brow, and opened her mouth and eyes.

I concentrated on holding her limp hand. I knew she was going to die and leave me. Did you know that when your heart breaks, it really feels like that? I thought I had a big crack all down the middle of my chest, it hurt so much.

Uncle Cavendish shook his head at last. "Yes, Your Majesty," he said heavily. "It is poison. From the yellow staining on the mat in the Withdrawing Chamber where she dropped the goblet, I am afraid it is darkwort." His face was quite grey because he had always liked my mother a lot.

"I have a piece of unicorn's horn in my cabinet," said the Queen, "and a bezoar stone."

"Alas, Your Majesty, not even they will help against essence of darkwort. It will not be long now . . ."

"I have called the Chaplain," the Queen told him.

They were speaking quietly but I heard them. I cried and put my arms round my mother as if I could hold her back. "Don't go," I whispered. "Stay with me, Mama. Please, stay . . ."

But she was too deep asleep to hear me.

I felt Uncle Cavendish standing behind me. "She has no pain," he said to me. "She can't feel anything now."

He might be a doctor, but I know that when I took my mother's hand to kiss it, I *know* I felt her grip my fingers to say goodbye. Then I kissed her face.

The Queen came and kneeled next to me and wrapped her arms round me and didn't mind when all my tears made her velvet bodice damp. She rocked me a little, silently, and I felt her crying, too.

My mother died at a little past midnight, St. Valentine's Day, 14 February 1568, the worst day of my whole life. I was only a babe when my father died serving the Queen in France, so I didn't really know about it. But my mother dying . . . I can't describe how terrible it was because I don't know enough long words, and anyway, I'm not a poet. It made a huge hole in the world.

Everyone has been kind to me over this last year, especially the Queen. She comforted me whenever I was really sad and promised me she would never send me away to be brought up by a stranger. Lord Worthy volunteered to be my guardian and administer my estates until I could marry and have a husband to do it for me. My Uncle Cavendish couldn't do it because he was ill, or so they told me. I think he is just drunk most of the time. He was always very fond of my mother and I don't think he has ever recovered from not being able to help her.

Oh yes, they found the poisoner. He was working for the dastardly Guises, who are always plotting the Queen's downfall. He tried to escape from the Queen's pursuivants and they killed him in the fight. The Queen was furious, though I don't think an execution would have made me feel any better.

By drinking Her Majesty's wine with the poison in it, my mother saved the Queen's life—and England from a terrible civil war like they have in France. That's why she is buried in Whitehall Chapel.

And now I shall take the courage to open the package.

Alas, I have made a blot in my daybooke—I'm afraid the package made me cry. As I opened it, a small leather purse fell onto the pillows. I left it there while I read my mother's letter. Half of it is in my mother's writing, with the letters getting bigger and more wobbly. Then it changes to the Queen's handwriting, which is sweeping and beautiful. There are two blots from tears at the end. That must be why Her Majesty was putting pen and ink away when Mrs. Champernowne brought me in that night. I will keep the letter here always, tucked in my daybooke.

> *My darling Grace,*
>
> *I am dying. My heart breaks that I shall not see you grow to womanhood, nor find you a fine man to take care of you and your estates.*
>
> *As you approach thirteen years, you must be found a husband soon. The Court, for all the Queen's kindness, is no place for a young maid. Her Majesty agrees and will take on the role of finding you a suitable match, so you may be handfasted and marry at sixteen.*
>
> *Rest assured that the Queen will do all that I*

would have done for you. You shall now have
my pearl ring that came from your father, and
all my gowns and horses. At your betrothal my
pearl earrings shall come to you.

You are the best of daughters, my love, and I
had rather anything than leave you so soon, but
none of us may gainsay God's call. I pray that
you will be happy and virtuous and always as
beloved as you are of me.

Farewell, my heart's delight, and at
Judgement Day be sure we shall meet again.

Until then my love is with you always.

Your mother,
Margaret, Lady Cavendish

I opened the leather purse. Inside were the earrings. They are beautiful pearl ones, with a setting of garnets and diamonds, like a pair the Queen often wears, only not so big.

Taking my candle, I went and looked in Lady Sarah's glass and put the hooks in my ears. As I stared at myself, and watched the garnets and diamonds glistening in the candlelight, I was reminded of my mother wearing them, and laughing.

Oh no, another teardrop blot. Time for bed.

Later this Day—
five of the clock from the chimes

It is still very dark outside. Something woke me up.
I am in bed, wearing my mother's earrings for comfort. Her letter is under my pillow. It is only paper
but it makes her feel closer, almost as if she's in the
room with me like she used to be when we shared a
chamber near the Queen's own. I hope I don't get
ink on the sheets.

The other two are still asleep in their bed. Lady
Sarah is still snoring like a pig, while Mary Shelton
is now snoring like a billy goat. But that isn't what
woke me. There is some kind of flurry over near the
Grace-and-Favour Chambers. I can hear hushed
voices, somebody running, lots of nervous whispers.
Nobody wants to wake the Queen, of course. She's
always bad-tempered in the morning, especially if it
was a late night.

There's definitely something interesting happen-
ing. I'm going to find out what it is.

Later this morn

I cannot believe it. I've never heard of such a thing.
A duel, perhaps—they happen sometimes and then

there's a scandal until it all dies down. But this! I can hardly write, my hand is shaking so much.

I have just told my bedfellows, Lady Sarah and Mary Shelton, and they've rushed off to look for themselves. I don't want to go back just yet because I need to think about something.

It seems hours ago that I got up, slipped a dressing gown over my smock, and put on my pattens, then clip-clopped out into the passageway. But it must only be five and twenty minutes or so. I thought the fuss was coming from the Grace-and-Favour Chambers, held by my Lord Worthy as a sign of the Queen's esteem, so I made my way there.

I didn't take a candle, I just crept along the stone floor, down the stairs, and along the passage. A crowd of people, wearing dressing gowns or clothes they'd thrown on hurriedly, were gathered round one of the doorways.

And there was poor Pip, white as a sheet, wringing his hands and stuttering. "I only went into my m-master's chamber so early to put out a bite of bread and beer for when he woke up, and I've n-n-never ever seen such a thing in all my d-days!"

It took a bit of quiet work with elbows and feet to get through—I'm tall enough, and being skinny and flat-chested is sometimes useful. Then I saw what had happened.

I didn't scream. Well, I did, but I had my hands to my mouth so it only made a squeak. At least I didn't swoon. That would be such a Lady Sarah thing to do. But my legs went all wobbly and my stomach turned inside out.

There was Sir Gerald, still in his velvet doublet, face down on the bed with the curtains pulled. And there was a dagger in his back!

In fact, it was the pretty dagger which had been his gift to me. I couldn't take my eyes off him. It wasn't that disgusting—there wasn't even any blood. It was just so shocking. My heart was banging *bam-da-da-bam* like French Louis's drum.

I'm not sure how long I stood and stared before I noticed that Sir Charles was in the room, by the bed, and so was Lord Robert, standing by the wall in his shirt and hose. He looked pale green.

There was a flurry and Lord Worthy arrived with four of his men, ploughing through to the front of the crowd and marching straight in. He stopped dead, staring at the bed. His usually rather grey and boring face was as white as the feathers of that nasty swan we'd eaten at the feast.

Pip kneeled. "My lord, I b-brought Sir Gerald's

breakfast early and s-saw . . ." He trailed off and just waved a hand helplessly.

Lord Worthy didn't seem to be listening properly; he was still staring at the pretty dagger in his nephew's back.

Then he gazed round, collecting his thoughts very slowly, as if somebody had scattered them all over the room and he was having to bend down and pick up each thought separately. After an age he began to speak. "First, double the guard on Her Majesty's bedchamber. When she wakes, please tell her what has occurred. Has Dr. Cavendish been sent for?"

"On his way, m'lord," said one of the men-at-arms of the Queen's Guard. "As this crime took place within the Verge of the Court, we must call my Lord Chamberlain and convene the Board of Green Cloth to hear the inquest."

Lord Worthy's face then crumpled and he held on to the pillar of the bed.

I felt so sorry for him, even though he had little time for me, despite being my guardian. I slid next to him and touched his arm.

He turned his head and looked at me, but I don't think he saw me. His hair was standing straight up and he looked quite exhausted—and quite slovenly for him. He hadn't even changed his shirt, which had a wine stain on the blackworked front and a greenish stain on the cuff.

He blinked at me, then shook his head and turned back to the corpse. "Did anyone see anything suspicious after my nephew left the St. Valentine's Ball?"

Pip started with how he had wanted to attend his master, and how he had gone in and hung up Sir Gerald's doublet but left his hose and canions so he could sleep off the drink, and how he had gone in specially early with bread and beer . . .

I noticed he had left out Ellie cleaning up Sir Gerald's vomit for him. I opened my mouth and took breath to point this out, and then I thought a bit: it might be better if Ellie's being there wasn't mentioned—it was impossible she could have stabbed Sir Gerald, but I was sure that the person who *had* would love to get an unimportant laundrymaid blamed for it!

My uncle Dr. Cavendish arrived then, wrapped in his brocade and marten dressing gown and rocking slightly. His face was puffy and his eyes bloodshot and he looked as if he wished his head would just get on with it and fall off. He even winced at the candle-light. Then he bent to examine Sir Gerald.

As he was doing so, Sir Charles pointed to a little silver shape lying next to Sir Gerald's hand on the pillow. "What is that?" asked Sir Charles sharply.

Dr. Cavendish picked it up and held it close to a candle. "It's an aiglet," he said. "Still with a bit of lace attached. Hmm. The crest . . ."

"That's not my master's," said Pip, peering at it closely. "Looks more like the Radcliffe crest."

"What?" snapped Lord Worthy, and everybody turned to stare at Lord Robert Radcliffe.

He stared back, going red, doing his usual thing of mouth-opening-but-nothing-coming-out.

"By God, you must have dropped it when you stabbed Sir Gerald!" shouted Sir Charles. "It's clear evidence."

"B-b-but . . . ," stammered Lord Robert desperately.

"Don't lie, sir—how else could your own aiglet come to be there?" demanded Sir Charles. "You were jealous of Sir Gerald's affections for your lady love—jealous enough to kill your rival while he slept."

"I . . ." Now Lord Robert grabbed for his sword hilt, but since it was not part of his night attire, he didn't have it with him. Lord Worthy's henchmen moved to either side of him.

"Aha!" said Sir Charles, standing four square in front of Lord Robert, waving his forefinger. "So now you threaten me? How long will it be before you come and stab *me* in *my* bed?"

It was no good, I had to say something. After all, he was my betrothed! "But, sirs," I said, "could not the killer have put the aiglet there on purpose to implicate my Lord Robert?"

They didn't hear me at all. They just went on shouting. Sir Charles and Lord Worthy really didn't like Lord Robert. Both looked delighted that they could blame him for the killing and present the Queen with the culprit as soon as she heard the news. It was so convenient, I knew nobody was going to listen to a young maid in her shift and dressing gown.

So I watched, feeling sick, while Lord Robert's arms were grabbed by Lord Worthy's men. Then he was officially told he was under arrest on suspicion of killing Sir Gerald, most dishonourably, while he slept.

Lord Robert stared back, white-faced. At least he had the sense not to talk. Then there was a pause while Lord Worthy tried to think where to put him. There are no dungeons at Whitehall, every scrap of space being needed by the Court. All the dungeons are downriver at the Tower. In the end they decided to put him in the basement of one of the Court Gate towers, in one of the storerooms there, which has barred windows.

Lord Robert didn't say anything when they took him away. Lord Worthy and Dr. Cavendish conferred to arrange the details of the inquest. It was decided that there didn't need to be an autopsy because it was obvious what had killed Sir Gerald—nobody survives a knife blade stuck deep into their back, even if it is a very pretty one with garnets on the hilt.

Suddenly it occurred to me that the blade could have been mine if I had chosen to marry Sir Gerald. Would I then have been charged with murder instead? That made me feel so sick, I turned and ran all the way back to my chamber.

When I got there Mary Shelton was sitting up in bed with her hair in curling papers and she looked at me curiously. "What are you doing out of bed, Grace?" she asked.

"The most extraordinary thing has happened," I told her excitedly. "There's been a murder at Court!"

Mary let out a little scream and Lady Sarah blinked slowly awake. "Wherefore are you making such a fuss and bother?" she asked irritably. "I'm trying to sleep."

"Oh, Sarah, dear," gasped Mary. "Really, you'll never guess. There's been a murder. Grace knows all about it."

Sarah snapped awake immediately. "Lord preserve us!" she exclaimed. "A murder? Not the Queen?"

"No, no, not the Queen," I assured her quickly, as I pulled my stays on over my head. "Somebody stabbed Sir Gerald in the back."

"How dreadful!" Sarah declared, looking downcast. "He is so charming and he dances well. Will he recover?"

"Unlikely. He is dead. It's very mysterious. They have arrested Lord Robert but I don't think he was the assassin. . . ."

That was that. By now, they weren't listening. I've never seen either of them dress themselves so fast and then they ran out of the door and down the passage. I wonder when Mary noticed she still had her curling papers in.

Poor Sir Gerald, I still can't believe he is really dead. One moment showing off to me in the Volta, the next moment—gone!

And as for my Lord Robert . . . I hate to think of him locked in some storeroom. The Queen will have him committed to the Tower if nobody does anything to find out the real murderer. I feel so sorry for him. Of all people who might have stabbed Sir Gerald, I really don't think it was he. Why should he? I'd agreed to marry him, hadn't I? Now if Sir Gerald had stabbed Lord Robert, that would have made sense. . . .

I must soon dress and make ready to serve the Queen at her rising. I do find that writing about things clears the head; if you set it down in black and white, you must think it through first. The Queen told me that and she is right—she is very wise. Aha! That's what I'll do to help Lord Robert. I'll speak to the Queen for him. At least she never tells me not to worry my pretty little head about things.

Later this Day—eventide

I am back in bed, writing this to keep myself awake. I have a plan, and it's very exciting, but I mustn't fall asleep if it is to work! After dressing this morning, I went along to serve the Queen at her rising, hoping she would be in a mood to talk. Everyone at Court knows if you want to talk to the Queen, you have to pick the right moment.

While I held the Queen's bodice straight for Lady

Bedford to sew the neckline into place, I got up courage to talk to her.

"Your Majesty," I began hesitantly. "May I talk to you about—"

"My Lord Robert?" The Queen had her lips compressed and looked very fierce. "Very well. But please remember that the aiglet lying on Sir Gerald's pillow was his."

"Indeed, Your Majesty!" I agreed. "But it makes no sense for Lord Robert to want to kill Sir Gerald over me, when I'd chosen him anyway! Is it possible that someone planted the aiglet, so that we should think the worst of poor Lord Robert?"

The Queen looked at me for a moment, while Lady Bedford tutted disapproval that I was being so cheeky.

Then the Queen said, "Hmm."

"At least don't commit him to the Tower yet," I begged. I kneeled and took her hand to kiss it. "Please, Your Majesty, may I . . . try and find out the truth of the matter?"

"Well, really, I don't think it's suitable . . . ," began Lady Bedford, but the Queen held up her hand.

"Very well. You may make discreet enquiries, Lady Grace," she said sternly. "But report your findings to me, and to no one else. Lord Robert can stay where he is for a day but after that I must commit him to the Tower, or release him."

"Thank you, Your Majesty. Um . . . may I . . . ?"

"What?" She was starting to sound seriously annoyed now, but I knew she was about to meet the Scottish and French Ambassadors and I couldn't bear the thought of sitting about on a cushion with incomprehensible French and Scotch whizzing about my head.

"Please may I walk the dogs?"

"Oh, go to!" she snapped. "By all means, I had rather have you out with them in the garden than wriggling about on a cushion distracting me."

"Thank you, Your Majesty, thank you!"

"*If* you can go upstairs and change your kirtle without making a thunder to wake the dead."

Honestly! Anyone would think I was made of lead. I ran upstairs as quietly as I could, changed into my hunting kirtle, wrapped a cloak around me, and then carried my boots down the stairs until I got to the door into the Privy Garden—where I astonished the guard there by pulling my boots on and lacing them, standing on one leg. One of the dog-pages brought me the dogs on their lead and we ran out into the garden, Henri in front, barking madly.

I went round the maze twice and then through

the gate into the Orchard, where I let the dogs off the lead and climbed my cherry tree to sit and think in a good sitting place—the crook between two branches. I could see where the buds were coming, but it was still too cold and wet for them to swell yet.

My head felt close to bursting with plans. I knew exactly how to find out the murderer: Uncle Cavendish once told me how much you can tell from a dead body. For instance, if you shine a light into the eyes, you might see an image of the murderer. And if you bring the true murder weapon near it, the body will bleed again. So it was obvious what I had to do—I needed to see Sir Gerald's body again.

I climbed down and went to explore the compost heaps. Ellie and Masou were there, bent over something on the ground. Eric rushed between them and tried to grab whatever it was, but Ellie snatched it up and held it out of reach while he bounced on his haunches, yapping.

"Ellie," I said, "why are you holding a half-skinned rabbit?"

"We are going to spit-roast it over a fire and eat it," Masou answered, as if this were perfectly obvious.

"And I'm going to peg out the skin and scrape it and cure it to make a muff for the winter," Ellie put in.

I tied up the dogs out of reach and squatted down to watch Ellie finish her work. She was very quick and deft. She had already taken off the paws, and she was peeling back the skin as if she was undressing it. It wasn't nearly as disgusting as you'd think because there wasn't any blood. The rabbit was already drawn and gutted.

And that's when the thought suddenly struck me: when I saw poor Sir Gerald with the dagger in his back, there hadn't been any blood around the wound! Which didn't make any sense because only *dead* bodies don't bleed—and surely Sir Gerald was alive when the dagger went in. It was one more mystery and one more reason why I needed another look at Sir Gerald's body.

"One of the kitchen spit-dogs caught it in the yard and broke its neck and I managed to get it off him," Ellie was explaining about the rabbit. "I gave him the guts. There now," she finished, handing the rabbit to Masou.

Masou had a long peeled twig, which he carefully threaded through the rabbit, and then he hung it over the fire, where it started to steam and cook. Ellie sprinkled some breadcrumbs over it while we began to discuss the murder.

There had been plenty of gossip and theories about it, one of which, Masou and Ellie told me, was that armed Scots had burst into the palace and murdered Sir Gerald in his bed in mistake for the Queen. I told them what had really happened and explained why it couldn't have been Lord Robert. I *did* have a moment's doubt, because I suddenly remembered Lord Robert saying that he hated Sir Gerald and reaching for his sword at the St. Valentine's Ball. But then I realized that that was just silly—Lord Robert would never have stabbed Sir Gerald in the back. I'm sure of it.

"Poor man," said Ellie ghoulishly. "He'll hang for a clean bill then."

"No, he won't," I said. "I'm not having my future husband hanged before I can even marry him—that would be stupid."

"But not so bad if it happened after the marriage?" asked Masou teasingly.

"At least then I'd be a proper matron," I sniffed.

"I'll go along and throw lavender and rue on the scaffold," said Ellie. "And I'll tell him how sad you are—that'll comfort him. And then I'll get the ballad-maker to invent a ballad and print it and—"

"Ellie, he's not going to hang because I'm going to find out what really happened," I told her severely.

Masou made a mock bow and turned the rabbit on its spit. "My lady, you are all-wise," he said. "Tell me, how will you do that?"

I punched him on the arm (not hard). "First I want to get a good long look at Sir Gerald's body," I began. "I've heard that it's being kept in St. Margaret's Chapel."

"Ugh," said Ellie. "Why?"

"Because when I saw Sir Gerald's body with the knife in it there wasn't any blood," I said very significantly.

"So?" frowned Masou.

"So, if I stabbed you, blood would come out, wouldn't it?" I explained. "Probably quite a lot if I stabbed deep enough to kill you. But there wasn't any blood around the wound and I remember my uncle, Dr. Cavendish, telling me once that the tides of your blood only stop when you die."

"Oh," murmured Masou thoughtfully.

"So I simply must look at Sir Gerald's body

again. And there's another reason, too." I lowered my voice because it was a frightening idea even if it was a well-known fact. "If we look into his eyes we might even be able to see who the murderer really was!"

"Why didn't the doctor do it when he saw the body?" asked Ellie matter-of-factly, munching on one of the marchpane arms of Venus that Masou had produced from his sleeve.

"Well, my uncle was upset," I said. "And he drinks too much, ever since . . . you know."

They both nodded.

"But I'm sure I've picked enough up from him to spot anything that might help," I went on.

Masou laughed. "So all we need to do is creep out to St. Margaret's Chapel at dead of night—"

"Yes, I was thinking *midnight,*" I put in. "Then we take a careful look at Sir Gerald's body, shine a light in his eyes, and we'll have the answer."

"Such simplicity that we must do it and nobody else has," Masou said, grinning.

I scowled at him. "Nobody else has because they all want it to be nice and simple. Lord Robert hasn't got a lot of friends and he owes people money and it would be simple if it were he," I explained.

"Not for the people he owes money to," Ellie pointed out.

"What about Lord Worthy's men, who will be guarding the chapel?" Masou asked quietly.

I hadn't thought about that. "You don't have to come with me," I told them. "I don't want you to get into trouble. I can find St. Margaret's Chapel on my own, you know."

"Oh, fie!" said Ellie. "I owe you one for not telling anybody that I cleaned up after Sir Gerald." She made a face. "Not a penny did I get for it, and his sick smelled horrible."

"And I," said Masou, "am a warrior and afraid of nothing—*and* I'm the best boy acrobat in Mr. Somers's troupe. They will require much worse of me before they turn me off, and if they do, why, I'll go to Paris Garden or the theatre and make my fortune."

"I'll go to the apothecary and get a sleeping draught," said Ellie, winking at me. "Maybe it will find its way into the guards' beer."

I kissed them both—Masou rubbed quickly at the side of his head where my kiss had landed. Then I gave Ellie some coins for the sleeping draught and rushed off to round up the dogs and take them back in for rubbing down by one of the dog-pages.

Which is why I happened to be at the stables talking to a groom when Sir Charles came wandering along, as he always does at that time of day. "Ah! Lady Grace," he said.

"Did we have a riding lesson today?" I asked, conscience-stricken that I might have forgotten it.

He looked bewildered and then said, "No, I think not. With all that has happened . . ."

"Well, at least let's go and say hello to Doucette," I suggested, because I didn't want him to be disappointed. "I'm sure she misses you, if not me."

"Hmm," he replied. He still seemed very uncertain, so I led him to Doucette's stable and unlatched the upper door. She put her pretty head out—I think she has some Welsh pony in her—and nickered to me. I patted her velvety nose and she blew.

Sir Charles reached out suddenly to pat her neck, and she jerked away, snorting and showing her teeth. He pulled back. "Good God, what's wrong with the nag?"

I stared with astonishment. Never ever in all my many (fairly dull) riding lessons with Sir Charles have I heard him talk of a horse that way, or indeed seen a horse react to him like that. It was astonishing.

I was going to ask what was wrong with *him*. How

could he forget everything he had told me about moving softly and slowly with horses? But then a dog-page came trotting up with the newly brushed dogs.

"My lady," he said breathlessly, "the Queen has called for you to take the dogs to her."

I guessed Her Majesty's Council meeting had tried her patience. She likes to play with the dogs when she's annoyed. I took the leads, said a hurried goodbye to Sir Charles, and rushed back to the Privy Gallery.

Just in time, I remembered to take my boots off before I went upstairs to change again (it is hellishly hard work to look smart and fitting for the Queen's magnificence). Then I lifted my skirts and raced up the stairs. As I reached the top, Mrs. Champernowne pounced.

"What are you doing, Lady Grace?"

"I'm going to change my kirtle again so I can attend Her Majesty properly attired," I said, quite sickly and sweet.

"Your stockings, child, look at your stockings!"

I looked down at where I was still holding up my skirts. Well, they had been a very nice pair of knitted white silk stockings but they were now a bit blackish around the feet and there was a hole in the toe of one and the knee of the other.

"Oh," I said, hastily dropping my hem to hide the offending garments. "I was trying not to make so much noise, Mrs. Champernowne, like you told me, and . . ."

She shut her eyes for a second, then looked up to the ceiling. "Lady Grace, boots are for— Wear your slippers while you— Oh, for goodness' sake, give me the stockings and go and put your woollen ones on. You cannot possibly attend the Queen with filthy stockings, look you . . ."

Very quickly, for she seemed near to bursting with annoyance at me, I stripped off the offending stockings, gave her the whole lot, along with garters, and ran barefoot along the passageway to my chamber to change again! Woollen stockings are a penance! They itch like mad! Why not go barelegged? Who can see your legs under all the petticoats and the far-thingale and so on? Ellie doesn't even own a pair of stockings and it doesn't seem to be killing her.

The Queen was in a terrible mood that afternoon. I sat near her while she petted the dogs and threw balls for them, and did some embroidery. Mary Shelton was then lunatic enough to slap crossly at Henri when he bounced over to lick her face.

"Out of my sight!" Her Majesty roared. I've left out her swearing because it's too rude to write down. "How dare you beat my dog? Out, you, and your sour, yellow looks . . ." And a hairbrush and a pot of lip balm whizzed past Mary's head as she ran for the door, ducking as she went.

I whispered to Lady Bedford, suggesting that maybe the tumblers might amuse. So they were sent for and we all watched Masou and a little old dwarf man and a strongman do somersaults and hand-stands and juggle with their feet. Masou then did a trick where he kept pretending to drop his balls and clubs and then caught them with his feet or his knees or his teeth and kept it all going, and that, at last, cheered the Queen up.

Since she felt sorry for him, Her Majesty invited Lord Worthy to share supper with her. And then she bade me join them, too. I really didn't want to—I was too nervous about the midnight plans to have much appetite for pheasant and salt beef and venison pasties. But I didn't have any choice.

Lord Worthy arrived late, looking flustered and still upset, and he still hadn't changed his shirt. Normally the Queen would have thrown a slipper at him for that, but she was being gentle with him because of his bereavement.

Lord Worthy decided to talk only to the Queen and only about terribly boring things like Scottish politics and French politics—it was all Guises and Maxwells and if so and so did this, then such and such would do the other thing. How anybody can keep it straight in their head is a mystery. I didn't mind. I was thinking about what we were going to do later in the night, wondering what I would wear and whether Ellie would manage to get the sleeping draught. I sat there looking as interested as I could, fighting the urge to yawn. At least there were some new Seville orange suckets, which I really love.

At last Lord Worthy ground to a halt.

Her Majesty put her hand out and touched his. "My lord, you will now have the estates belonging to Sir Gerald to administer as well as your own and Lady Grace's," she said softly.

Lord Worthy looked bleakly at her. "I have a very good steward, Your Majesty," he replied. "We shall manage."

"Of course," Her Majesty agreed. "And of yourself, my lord?" she continued gently. "I know how highly you rated your nephew."

"I did, Your Majesty. He was a fine young man—

with a young man's faults, true. He was hasty-tempered, inclined to sarcasm when crossed, certainly arrogant, but I believe time would have mended those faults as it normally does."

"Well," said the Queen, blinking at the dullness of Lord Worthy's voice, "we shall commit young Lord Robert to trial in a day or two."

Lord Worthy nodded sadly, still staring at the candle flame.

I watched him curiously. It had suddenly occurred to me that he might be almost as sad about his nephew dying as I was about my mother dying. My eyes suddenly prickled.

The Queen could see there was no cheering him up, and so she went over to her virginals, which stood in the corner of her Withdrawing Room, lifted the lid, and began tuning them. The Queen is very musical. She played some beautiful Italian music which made me feel much better—I really like listening to her play. Even ambassadors do; you can see them tense up as she gets ready to start and then smile and relax because they can actually tell the truth and be complimentary at the same time.

Lord Worthy sat politely and I got the impression he was waiting to talk to the Queen on his own, so as another song came to an end, I rose and curtsied and asked to be excused to go to my bed. The Queen kissed me goodnight on the cheek and I went upstairs quite slowly, feeling sorry for Lord Worthy.

The other girls weren't there yet, they were playing cards in the Presence Chamber, but Ellie was sitting on my bed looking very perky.

"How did it go?" I asked her. "Did you get the sleeping draught?"

"Yes. You gave me lots of money—look, I got a whole bottle of laudanum for it." She held up a small green bottle. "I got all wrapped up in a striped cloak and went to an apothecary in Westminster."

I looked sideways at her. "Where did you get a striped cloak?" (Only harlots wear them—it's a sort of uniform for them. The City Fathers make them do it.)

"Oh, we do a little extra laundry on the side," Ellie said casually, "and one of the strumpets at the Falcon got a new one when we were washing hers, so she didn't bother to collect it, said we could keep it. It comes in quite useful sometimes."

I nodded.

"Here's the change." Ellie dropped the coins on my bed. "Now remember not to drink any of the wine on the sideboard there—I've put several drops of laudanum in it so the two twitter-heads will sleep well."

Ellie can't bear most of the Maids of Honour, which is hardly surprising, considering how rude they are to her when she collects their dirty linen.

"Me and Masou will meet you by the kitchen," she continued, "an' if you don't turn up by the time the moon is over the trees in the Orchard, we'll go and 'ave a look at Sir Gerald ourselves. He's already in St. Margaret's Chapel but I don't think he's laid out yet—they need to do the inquest first."

Ellie hopped off the bed, gathered up a couple of smocks lying in a twist on the floor and one ruff that had been stamped on, stuffed them in her bag, and headed off down the passageway. So I cleaned my teeth, changed into my hunting kirtle, pulled a smock on over the top of it, and here I am. And now, at last, I can hear Lady Sarah and Mary approaching. Soon I will set off on my midnight adventure.

For now, I will pretend to be asleep.

*Eventide, just past five of
the clock from the chimes*

Lord preserve me, I am in the most terrible trouble. I hardly dare think how angry the Queen was. At least, as I am sent to my bedchamber in disgrace, I can write this.

To begin where I left off. Last evening, the two twitter-heads came back quite late, about ten of the clock. They had been playing Primero and were arguing over who had given her point-score wrong. Olwen, their tiring woman, helped them out of their gowns. They glugged some of the drugged wine after they'd cleaned their teeth and got into their beds, still arguing about the Primero game. I gathered they'd lost to Mrs. Champernowne.

Olwen bustled about hanging things up and brushing things and folding things until I wanted to shake her, and then she left, at last. Very soon, I could hear the twitter-heads snoring.

I waited impatiently for the guard to change at midnight outside the Queen's Privy Gallery. When I'd heard the changeover I slid out of bed, leaving the curtains closed, and pulled off my smock. I'd already left my horrible wool stockings off. Then I crept out of the door and down the passageway, dodging into a doorway when a cat came past with a mouse in her mouth.

The first frightening part was climbing out of a window into the Privy Garden. That bit over, I slunk through the gate into the Orchard: it was kept locked, but I knew that the gentleman who held the key hid it under a stone next to the gate so he didn't lose it. I went through the Orchard to the compost heaps, where Ellie and Masou were waiting for me.

Ellie was already wearing boy's clothes—borrowed from one of the women at the laundry whose son had died of plague the year before, she said, which made me shiver. She'd brought another set for me, but I refused to wear them. Only people like Ellie, who've already had plague and got better, aren't scared of it, because you can't get it twice.

Masou shrugged. "If we are caught, my lady, it

will go better for us if they can see you are one of the Queen's women," he said.

I didn't really want to hear about that because I think half the fun of a midnight adventure is getting disguised. I frowned. "I'll have to wear my kirtle then," I concluded. There was nothing else for it. I could hardly climb the Orchard wall in my shift.

We climbed over the compost heap and the old bean staves covered in bindweed, and found the bit of wall that's crumbling. Masou had brought a rope to help us and we scrambled over.

The next courtyard was behind a row of houses that were rented by the room to the young gentlemen of the Court. It was a mess of brambles, beer barrels, broken horn mugs, broken clay pipes, tables, a broken lute, half a dozen chairs that must have been in a fight, and a piece of petticoat caught on a nail halfway up a wall.

We crept through the clutter, with Masou muttering in his own language when he caught himself on a thorn; then we slid along an alleyway that gave into New Palace Yard. Westminster Abbey loomed over us as we passed through the gate leading to the chapel where Sir Gerald's body lay.

Masou crept ahead noiselessly to see if any of Lord Worthy's men were still awake.

"They'll be snoring," whispered Ellie behind me. "I found 'em hanging about waiting for his lordship to finish supping with the Queen, so I took their flasks down to the buttery for 'em. Aqua vitae and laudanum. Wasn't that kind and serviceable of me?" She grinned.

Masou crept back, his white teeth shining in the moonlight. "Sleeping like babes."

We picked our way past them—they were rather sweetly propped up against each other on a bench inside the church porch—and carefully, carefully opened the heavy wooden door into the chapel.

There were six black corpse candles around the body, which had been wrapped in a shroud and was laid on a trestle table covered with damask. No doubt a very special elaborate coffin was on order but it hadn't arrived yet.

It was very cold and very frightening. The moon was shining through the old Papist stained-glass windows, making pale blues and yellows on the shroud, and there was a nasty smell. Ellie shivered and crossed herself, while Masou clutched a little amulet he wears round his neck and muttered in his own language.

I gulped, stepped forward, and nearly tripped on a step. Heart beating fast, I then went right up to the body. Up close, the smell was truly awful, a bit like an unemptied close-stool. But there was something else as well: another, much fainter odour—dusty and bitter, it caught inside my nose. Curiously, it made me want to cry. Why? I didn't understand it. Although it's sad when someone dies, I certainly hadn't loved Sir Gerald.

He was lying on his back—they'd taken the knife out of the wound, of course. I held my breath and slowly drew the shroud back from his face.

There were pennies on the eyes to hold them shut. I took them off. The lids were half opened. His eyes were like jelly. I held a candle close, but I could see no reflection of a murderer in Sir Gerald's eyes. I wanted to look at the dagger wound again, but I didn't want to actually touch the corpse in case I was cursed. I reasoned with myself that Sir Gerald's ghost should be pleased we were trying to discover his murderer. But then I remembered that Sir Gerald wasn't a very nice man in life, so you could hardly expect his ghost to be. And then I noticed a slight yellow crusting at the corners of his mouth.

I blinked in surprise. My heart began to thud. That same yellow crusting had been on my mother's lips when she died. Now I knew where I'd smelled the dusty bitter odour on Sir Gerald. I had smelled it at my mother's deathbed. The smell of darkwort poisoning.

I stood for a moment, trying to understand. It seemed lunatic, but what if Sir Gerald had already been killed by darkwort poison when he was stabbed with the dagger? That would account for his not bleeding when stabbed, would it not? For if he was already dead, the tides in his blood would have stopped, and thus no blood would have streamed from the dagger wound.

Suddenly there was the sound of voices and heavy footsteps. Masou and Ellie and I froze, staring at each other. There was a scrape at the church porch, an angry shout. The door latch rattled. They were coming in.

I felt so sick I thought I was actually going to vomit, and my legs felt as if they would bend sideways like a rag doll's. Ellie had her hands to her mouth. Masou looked grey. Both of them would get really badly beaten if anybody saw them—especially Masou. Lord save us, they might even flog him properly! Both of them might be dismissed from the Queen's service, they would probably starve—whatever Masou said about making his fortune in Paris Garden. Whereas if I got caught . . .

"Hide," I whispered. "I'll manage this."

They hesitated, then slipped into one of the box pews. I could hear scraping as they hid under the bench.

I stayed exactly where I was near the body of Sir Gerald and started to cry. I don't find it easy to cry when I want (though Lady Sarah and Mary Shelton seem to find it so. They often grizzle to win sympathy and favour). But as soon as I thought about getting birched, or the Queen telling me off (which would be worse), the tears came. I helped them along by sniffing hard and sobbing and pinching my fingers on the middle of my nose.

The chapel door was thrust open and the guards marched in, along with Lord Worthy. They all looked very fierce—but, as I'd hoped, they came to a halt in the aisle when they saw me, sobbing by the body of my dead suitor.

Lord Worthy hurried forward looking flustered, and perhaps a little suspicious. "Well . . . well . . . Why did you not just *ask* to pay your respects, my lady? And why at night? It would have been far more . . . fitting . . . for you to come during the day, properly attended . . ."

"I . . . I wanted . . . to be alone with him," I

gulped, giving the performance my all. "I didn't want people flapping handkerchiefs at me."

"But how did you get here? Did someone help you?" Lord Worthy demanded.

"No, no!" I shrieked, terrified in case he searched the chapel. "I came all by myself, and it was very frightening."

Lord Worthy paused, staring blankly at Sir Gerald's corpse. I stood there, thinking how very hard-hearted of Lord Worthy not to try to comfort me. He is supposed to be my guardian, after all!

"Come, now, my lady," he said at last. "This is all highly unsuitable. With no escort . . . It is really very improper. I shall have to accompany you back to Court myself and hand you into Mrs. Champernowne's care."

Oh no! I thought. I hung my head and sobbed quite genuinely now.

"Come along," he said. He took my arm, pinching a bit, and led me out of the chapel by the other door, followed by his henchmen, who were gawking at me as if I had grown a bear's head. They clearly didn't know what to make of it all.

We walked through the churchyard and up through another gate into King's Street. On we went through King's Street Gate, and entered the palace at the end of the Privy Gallery. There, Lord Worthy spoke to the two gentlemen on guard. One of them walked off, looking highly amused.

We stood there, Lord Worthy tutting to himself and playing with a handkerchief in his pocket, me changing from one leg to the other. My heart would have been in my boots if I'd been wearing any. But I wasn't. I was wearing an old pair of dancing slippers. I really hoped Masou and Ellie had had a chance to get away from the chapel. I thought I'd seen a dark shape flit behind us as we went through the courtyard, but I wasn't sure.

After what seemed like ages, Mrs. Champernowne appeared in the door, her hair in curling papers, dressing gown wrapped around her against the cold. There was a mixture of astonishment and fury on her face, which would have been very funny if it had been aimed at somebody else.

"What is the meaning of this, Lady Grace?" she snapped.

I just muttered and stared at the ground.

"Out of bed, at this time of night . . . Was there any sign of a young man?" Mrs. Champernowne demanded of Lord Worthy suspiciously.

"No, there wasn't!" I shouted. "I was visiting the corpse of my—"

"That's enough," snapped Mrs. Champernowne. "When I wish to hear your lies, my lady, I shall ask for them."

"Mrs. Champernowne, I can vouch that there was no young man," said Lord Worthy. "There was no one else in the chapel."

"Hmph," said Mrs. Champernowne. Then she turned to Lord Worthy. "Thank you so much, my lord, for rescuing Lady Grace from her silliness . . ." She simpered disgustingly.

"Hmph," I said.

Lord Worthy bowed, Mrs. Champernowne curtsied. He and all his men went off towards the Grace-and-Favour Chambers while she grabbed my arm and pulled me upstairs behind her, pinching nastily as she went. "If I find out there *was* a young gentleman . . ."

"You can use a strap on my bare bum, Mrs. Champernowne!" I said hotly, furious that they thought I was no better than any other twitter-head. "Do you think I'm as stupid as Lady Sarah?"

"Lady Sarah has not been found in St. Margaret's Chapel at three in the morning where she had no business to be," Mrs. Champernowne pointed out.

"Not yet," I muttered; luckily, Mrs. Champernowne didn't hear. "I know it was foolish but I wanted to . . . um . . . say goodbye to Sir Gerald and I didn't want to be surrounded by chattering fools when I did and so I climbed a couple of walls and went to do it privately, and there most certainly wasn't any young gentleman anywhere near"—there was Masou, of course, but he's not a gentleman, so this was quite true—"and I didn't do anything wrong."

"You were not in your bed when you should have been, and you were where you should not have been," snapped Mrs. Champernowne—rather confusingly, I thought. "How dare you abuse Her Majesty's trust in you, how dare you sneak around like . . ." Then she took hold of herself. "Well now," she finished, "we will not bandy words like a couple of fishwives . . ."

Bit late for that, I thought. You must have woken half the Court with all that burbling, you old dragon.

At the top passageway she decided it was too late for me to retire to bed again and too early to tell the Queen, so she locked me in her little dressing room.

It was very dark and very stuffy and smelled rather

strongly of Mrs. Champernowne and rose-water and lavender water and a very expensive jasmine oil she gets from the east, which made the air almost too thick to breathe. I think she was hoping I would stand there stewing over what was going to happen in the morning, but I was really too exhausted. So I sat down on the rush matting, leaned my head in a corner, and went to sleep.

Hell's teeth! I must go and find more ink.

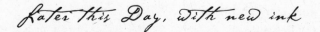

Later this Day, with new ink

Lady Sarah always keeps some ink new-made in her dressing table so I took that. She'll never notice.

In the morning I was shaken awake by Mrs. Champernowne, who seemed just as furious. I didn't get any breakfast and was told that Her Majesty would see me in the Presence Chamber, so I had to trot along behind Mrs. Champernowne in my grubby old hunting kirtle, all muddy from climbing walls. I kept thinking about Ellie and Masou. I really hoped they got away.

In the Presence Chamber the other Maids of Honour were sitting in a row on cushions, sewing— Lady Sarah I'm-so-pretty Bartelmy was mending a tear in one of her petticoats.

The Queen wasn't on her throne, but the chair she was sitting in by the window had a cloth of estate over it, so it was sort of official. I went towards her when she beckoned me, and then stopped three paces away and went down on both knees.

Her Majesty has pale skin but very dark brown eyes which sometimes seem to be able to reach out and dig right into your head. They were doing that now. I looked down, trying not to feel grubby and insignificant. She let me kneel there in silence for a long time and then . . .

"*What* in the name of *God* happened last night?" she shouted. "Have you run wood-wild? God's blood, I never heard the like!" And so on, swearing shockingly—which I have left out to save her reputation. Finally she ran out of ways of repeating that I'd been found in that cursed chapel by Lord Worthy. "Well, Lady Grace?" Her fingers rapped the arm of her chair. "What is your explanation?"

I sighed, feeling very tired. I also had a crick in my neck. But at least there was no sign that Masou or Ellie had been caught. If they had been, they would have been there in the Presence Chamber, too. That made me feel a lot better.

"We are waiting for an answer," said Her Majesty coldly.

"Um . . . I wanted to . . . um . . . well, look at Sir Gerald one last time," I offered.

"Why?" Her Majesty demanded rightly.

"I'm so sorry, Your Majesty, I just did." I looked up.

"And did you at least pray?" the Queen enquired.

"No, Your Majesty, I didn't have time. Lord Worthy came."

"Hmph." There seemed to be frustration in every inch of the Queen's body. "Lord Worthy tells me that there was nobody else in the chapel and that he feels sure you were not there for any immoral reason . . . But for the sake of your reputation, Lady Grace, you must *not* behave like this. It is not seemly in any young heiress and most certainly not in anyone in my service."

"No, Your Majesty," I replied quietly.

Finally the Queen said, "You will return to your chamber, Lady Grace, and remain there until I send for you. Perhaps you are overwrought with the strain of the St. Valentine's Ball and what took place afterwards. I shall ask Dr. Cavendish to attend you there and be sure that you are not sickening for anything."

I kept my head down, wondering if the Queen was really as angry as she appeared. And then I heard Her Majesty sigh and she leaned forwards to speak quietly in my ear. I saw some of the Ladies-in-Waiting looking over at us curiously, but they couldn't hear what she said.

"See now, Grace, you have put me in a most trying position. I cannot be seen to countenance such wild behaviour," she whispered. "You must try to be a little more discreet in your investigations." Then she called for Mrs. Champernowne to take me back upstairs to my chamber.

Back in my room, I sat on the bed, hugely relieved that I still had Her Majesty's support. Though, sadly, she seemed to have forgotten that I had not breakfasted. I sat listening to my stomach gurgle and wondered what to do next.

Thankfully, one of the tiring women brought me some bread and cheese and beer at midday. By that time I had washed off the mud, changed into my third-best kirtle, and was doing some embroidery by the little window. I started off hating needlework when my mama began to teach me. The sampler I first practised on seemed boring and pointless. But as I got better at it, I found I was able to draw pictures onto the white linen and then colour them in with silken threads. I find embroidering wonderful peacocks and singing birds and snakes and bears and horses a great comfort.

As the afternoon light faded, I had to stop because I couldn't see well enough. I stamped around the room, feeling that awful itchiness under my ribs that you get when you're bored. I would even have been quite pleased to see Lady Sarah and Mary Shelton. Then I thought of my daybooke and so I lit a candle and I have spent all this time writing and not caused very much mess. I'd better stop. There's someone at the door.

Later this Day, not long gone seven of the clock from the chimes

It was Masou and Ellie! We hugged each other. Masou kept shaking his head and saying something in his own language so Ellie tutted at him.

"Did they birch you?" asked Ellie anxiously. "Is your bum sore? I brought some comfrey ointment in case . . ."

"No, no," I told her, smiling. "It's all right. I didn't get any kind of beating. I've just been sent to my room until the Queen asks for me."

"Did you see anything in Sir Gerald's eyes?" asked Masou eagerly.

"No, but I did see something else," I told them. "There was a yellow stain on Sir Gerald's lips and a nasty bitter smell about him and I remember that . . ." I stopped. I hated what came into my mind when I said that. "I remember it from . . . from when my . . ." I stopped again and swallowed hard. "That's what killed my mother. Poison that made yellow froth on her mouth, that smelled bitter."

"Yes," said Ellie slowly. "And there was the same stuff in the sick I cleaned up from the mat in his chamber. A nasty yellow stain—I couldn't get it out by candlelight and I tried ten-day-old urine on it yesterday, and it still wouldn't come out."

They use disgusting things to clean with at the laundry—I sometimes can hardly believe what Ellie tells me. For bad stains? Dog dirt so old it goes white, for instance!

"They had to put a new piece of matting in where my mother dropped the wine cup," I said heavily, "because they couldn't get the stain out."

"But if he was dead by the poison, why stab him with the knife?" asked Masou.

He and Ellie both looked at me. "To confuse everybody? To make sure?" I suggested.

None of us could work it out. I told them I was probably not supposed to have any visitors and they should go, so Ellie picked up a very dirty shift of

Lady Sarah's and they went out again. What I think is that

This same Day,
nine of the clock from the chimes

I had to stop again and put my pillow over everything, as my uncle, Dr. Cavendish, arrived. I hope it isn't too blurred. There's a little ink on the pillowcase, though.

Since my mother died, I have only ever seen my father's brother in one of two states: drunk or hung over. He was hung over now—bloodshot eyes, grey face, miserable. He sighed and told me to sit on the bed and then he looked into my eyes and ears and mouth, put his ear to my chest, and then sat there quietly taking my pulses. There are twelve pulses, apparently.

Then he asked me questions, some of them very embarrassing, and when I told him "no" to all of them, he looked very puzzled.

"I would have said you were too young for the green sickness," he said. "There's no sign of fever, no sign of too much bile."

"That's because I'm not ill," I told him. And nor

did I want to be ill—I hate being bled—and as for purging . . . Lord preserve me!

"Then what possessed you to do such a foolish thing, Grace?" he asked. "If you were some silly minx like Lady Sarah then I would not even need to ask, but you are normally such a sensible, level-headed girl."

Am I? How boring, I thought. "I'm sorry that you should have seen so ugly a sight as a man killed with a dagger in his back while he slept," Uncle Cavendish went on, "and more than sorry that it should have been done by your own betrothed. But you cannot let this sad business turn your head, Grace—"

"But, Uncle, Sir Gerald wasn't killed by that knife," I interrupted.

He gave me a weary smile. "And what makes you say that, Dr. Grace, eh?"

"Uncle, there was no blood," I explained. "If you get stabbed by a knife, blood comes out."

My uncle just stared at me.

"Don't you remember telling me, Uncle?" I asked patiently. "You said that the heart is the body's furnace and the lungs are the bellows for the furnace. And the blood—the sanguine humour, you called it—carries the vital heat from the furnace to every part of the body, ebbing back and forth like tides."

"That's right," my uncle agreed.

"But if the tides had stopped because the man was dead, there would be no waves of blood to flow from the wound," I pointed out. "And I saw the dagger in Sir Gerald's back and there was *no blood,* was there? You saw it, too," I urged.

My uncle nodded.

"So that's why I wanted to go to the chapel," I hurried on. "To see if I could see the murderer's reflection in Sir Gerald's eyes and solve the mystery. I did not. But, Uncle, when I was in the chapel I noticed something else about the body." My voice shook. "There was a faint spot of yellow scum in the corner of his mouth and a bitter smell."

"You mean . . ." He blinked hard, swallowed. "Grace, just because your mother . . ." He felt absent-mindedly in his doublet, no doubt for his flask, which goes everywhere with him. I put my hand on his to stop him.

He stared at me for so long I thought he was angry, but then he spoke very softly. "I'm sorry, Grace, I should have noticed these things myself."

"Go and look, you'll see," I pressed him. "You've not had a surgeon open the body—you could if you asked. . . ."

"On the contrary, I asked and my Lord Worthy refused. . . ." My uncle spoke slowly and thoughtfully. "But I will go now and take a closer look at the body." He kissed me on the cheek, smelling rather sour himself, and then hurried from the room.

Lady Sarah and Mary Shelton have just returned. I am very tired, probably from not getting enough sleep last night; saving an innocent man is exhausting work! I shall stop writing now and prepare for bed.

I am writing this hurriedly, before I am summoned to attend the Queen at supper. I have had the most exciting day! And what we discovered! I can hardly believe it, though I heard it with my own ears. I should probably write this in orange juice—it's very secret—only I can't because of the marmelada. Also I need more ink and a new quill—mine is quite worn down with all my writing and it won't sharpen properly any more.

When Lady Sarah and Mary Shelton came back last night there was a lot of tutting and sighing over a couple of broken pots and a small tear in the curtain. Well, what was I supposed to do? It was so *dull* being in my chamber all evening, and I just wondered if I could get all the way round without touching the floor, which led to a slight accident with Lady Sarah's pots of face paint and Mary's bed curtains.

This morning the Queen sent for me. She told

me privately that she would have to commit Lord Robert to the Fleet Prison. It's supposed to be a bit better than the Tower, so I hope he won't be too miserable there. She also said that I might now leave my room and continue my investigation, as long as I was present to attend her at supper.

Relieved, I returned to my chamber and changed into my hunting kirtle. Then I went in search of Ellie, taking with me a spare pork pasty I had saved her from my supper.

Mrs. Twiste, who's in charge of the laundry, had set her scrubbing out the huge boiling bucks at the back of the laundry and she was just finishing when I found her.

"I've got an errand next," she said to me as I sat on the wall and watched her gobble the pasty in two bites. It was a cold frosty morning and her cheeks and nose were bright red. She gulped down the last crumbs and added, "I've got to take a pile of sheets to Mrs. Twynhoe. Would you like to help?"

Officially, Mrs. Twynhoe's married to the Naper's Deputy, who looks after the household linen, so she's in charge of all the bedlinen. But really she's a midwife and a wise-woman. I'd always wanted to meet her. "Is she really a witch?" I asked eagerly.

"No, she ain't a witch," Ellie replied. "She's a

lovely person and she knows all there is to know about herbs and potions. So we can ask her where somebody could have got darkwort from."

It was a pity about her not being a witch—I'd always wanted to ask one if they can really fly. But I was still very curious to meet Mrs. Twynhoe, so I went with Ellie to deliver the sheets.

Well, Mrs. Twynhoe was a real disappointment. She didn't even have any warts! She was a short, round person with a beaming face and soft grey curls under her cap and she had arms like a sailor's. She took the baskets from us as if they didn't weigh anything and put them on the long wooden rollers they use to help smooth out the linen.

"Mrs. Twiste said I should stay to help you if you needed it, Mrs. Twynhoe," said Ellie with a little bob.

Mrs. Twynhoe beamed even wider. "Oh, there now, of course you can, my dear. And call me Mrs. Bea—Twynhoe is such a mouthful, I couldn't even say it properly meself on my wedding day. If you could help me roll the sheets once I have the steam working, perhaps your friend could hem a sheet for me—I've just put it sides-to-middle and it needs a good needlewoman."

She gave me a thimble and a needle and a skein of

thread and an enormous linen sheet already pinned and then she and Ellie set to work stretching the sheets over the rollers using hot-metal irons from a small brazier. It looked very difficult and skilled and Ellie was impressively efficient. The big airing room soon got hot and steamy. I was sitting by the window stitching at the sheet as nicely as I could. I wondered how she knew to give me that job and then I thought she had probably seen me often enough, following the Queen in procession, and I just hadn't noticed her.

Ellie was chatting away to her about herbs and I listened carefully. "Half the soapwort in the kitchen garden got eaten by some nasty fly," she said. "We're having to buy it in from my Lord Worthy's gardens on the Strand."

"Oh, that's a nuisance. Did they plant it in among garlic and carrots?" asked Mrs. Bea.

Ellie shook her head. "The new Head Gardener likes things in straight rows and squares and he hates mixing plants in the same bed."

"More fool him then," said Mrs. Bea wisely. "Garlic is a charm to protect against blackfly."

"Mrs. Bea, Lady Grace wanted you to tell her what you know about darkwort," said Ellie finally.

Mrs. Bea's jolly red face suddenly looked serious. "That's nasty stuff, my dear. No good is ever done with darkwort." Mrs. Bea's eyes suddenly became like the Queen's—sharp enough to make a hole in your head. "And why are you so curious about dark-wort?" Then she suddenly remembered my mother. "Oh, my dear . . ."

"Mrs. Bea, I've reason to believe that Sir Gerald Worthy died of it the day before yesterday," I put in.

Mrs. Bea stopped smoothing the linen sheet. "Do you now?"

"Yes. I know because I recognized the faint yellow froth on his lips and that bitter smell," I replied.

"Hmm." Mrs. Bea stared very hard at me and then at Ellie and then took the newly-smooth sheet off the rollers and folded it up with Ellie's help, speaking as she did so. "Darkwort is a herb, related to belladonna or deadly nightshade. It's very rare. If dried and pounded, it makes a poisonous powder with no taste, though when mixed with certain sub-stances—wine, for instance—it stains yellow."

"Where might somebody get hold of darkwort?" I enquired.

Looking thoughtful, Mrs. Bea went and poured herself some mild ale out of a jug on the table by the door, offering us some as well. Ellie has never been known to turn down food and drink, and I had some because the heat in the room had made me thirsty. It was very good, better than I'd expected, flavoured with preserved lemon peel.

"Now then," Mrs. Bea said, sitting down and smoothing out her apron. "Perhaps four apothecaries in London might sell it. It is very expensive. At least ten shillings for a scruple."

"Which apothecaries are they?" I asked.

Mrs. Bea smiled at me. "I think I should not give you reason to run gallivanting around London town asking what villain has bought darkwort recently, even to save your future husband," she said.

I sighed. "How can I do it then?"

"Marry, I shall go and ask them myself," said Mrs. Bea stoutly. "And they're more likely to tell me the truth than you, my dear, since they know me. And then I shall tell you."

She was being so helpful I decided to risk it. "Thank you, Mrs. Bea," I said carefully. "And what's also really needed is for someone to look around the chambers of people like my Lord Robert, quietly, without alarming them . . ."

"And find if there's darkwort powder?" Mrs.

Bea's bright eyes were considering me. "Hmm. How is the sheet coming along?"

"Hm? Oh, I've finished. It was only plain sewing," I replied.

She took the sheet from me and looked at the hem very critically, then nodded her approval. "I think you and Ellie might have a little free time now. I'll tell Mrs. Twiste I sent you in search of some pillow-slips and sheets that are missing." She dug in a chest. "Here's a white cap and apron so you look the part, my dear."

Ellie smiled and curtsied and so did I because she was kind and she didn't have to help us, did she? Then we took the linen bag and rushed out and down the passage.

I was glad of the cap and apron—they would be a useful disguise in case we met anyone who knew me. I put them on. Ellie explained that when fetching things from the courtiers' chambers she was always sent with someone, partly to prevent any pilfering, partly to make sure no one treated her badly. Both Mrs. Twiste and Mrs. Bea had dim views of the average gentleman.

We made our way down to the next floor, which is the Long Gallery, above the Queen's Apartments. It sounded as if elephants were galloping about in there. Ellie stopped me going in and we hid at the bend of the stairs to listen to the musicians playing the drum and viol while the Maids of Honour practised their dancing. The Dancing Master was wailing as usual, "And two and one and leap . . ." There was a thunderous series of thuds. "Like a feather!" shrieked the dancing master. "On the toes! *Mon Dieu, ce sont les vaches . . . vraiment . . .*"

Ellie giggled and so did I. After a minute the music stopped and there was a rush of footsteps on the stairs, followed more slowly by the Dancing Master and one of the musicians, both drinking from little flasks.

When they had all gone we entered and found Masou standing gravely on his hands and walking up and down—he had been roped in to provide a partner for girls who needed to practise.

"No, I cannot come," he said to us when we told him what we were going to do. "Mr. Somers wants me to be able to walk on my hands and juggle with my feet and I must practise for a new tumble he has made." He went up and down again, looking as if he could walk to York like that. "And also, laundrymaids may poke about in chambers but if I should be found there, they'll think I was thieving."

So we left him and made our way to the Grace-and-Favour Chambers to begin our search. The first place we went was my Lord Robert's chamber. I had to be sure, before we looked elsewhere. One of his men was sitting by the door, playing a game of cards. He looked very depressed.

Ellie marched right up to him. "Mrs. Twynhoe wants me to find some sheets and pillowslips," she said.

The man shrugged and opened the door. I slipped in quickly, carefully hiding my face, and Ellie followed. We found quite a small, odd-shaped chamber, with a bed with four tall carved corner posts, and a truckle bed, and more mess than you would believe possible. The floor was covered with chicken leg bones, half-chewed sausages, bits of paper, and dirty hose. I was fascinated. It was nearly as bad as a Maid of Honour's chamber.

We discovered pots of ointment, with prescriptions from my Uncle Cavendish stating that they would prevent skin blemishes. Our hearts thudded when we found packets of herbs secreted in a chest amongst Lord Robert's hose. Ellie picked up a note that was with them and handed it to me to read. It was in my uncle's writing. He had prescribed a potion to cure a stammer. *"Boil marigolds, agrimony, and borage in posset drink, sweeten it with sugar, and let* the patient drink it going to bed," I read out loud. Poor Lord Robert. It clearly hadn't worked.

Nowhere did we find a yellow powder that might be darkwort. I did discover, however, why Lord Robert was so poor. It seemed he was always losing money at cards to other courtiers, and losing more at dice in the City inns. One small chest was almost full of bills and letters about debts. He seemed to owe money to everybody I'd ever heard of, and plenty I hadn't.

There was also a letter, written but not finished, from Lord Robert to his Lady Dowager mother, dated 14 February:

> *Dearest Mother,*
> *You will be pleased to know that I have at last managed to make a good match, thanks to the Queen's kind offices, and your good advice. I expect to be out of debt as soon as I am handfasted to the heiress of the Cavendishes. As you predicted, beloved Mother, she liked pearls better than any of the other gifts on offer, they being a flask and a knife. Luckily, I find her not too foul-visaged, although hardly begun to own womanly curves, being rather skinny. She seems virtuous and*

cheerful and her worst vice is that she talks
constantly. No doubt time will improve her greatly.

"Huh!" I said, feeling very hurt. I'd thought the pearls meant Lord Robert had found out what jewels I like best; but no, he'd asked his mother what girls like. And worse, much worse, he'd only been interested in my estates. How disgustingly unromantic. And who was he to say I was "not too foul-visaged" and talked too much? Better than not being able to talk at all, *I* think.

I didn't tear the letter up, although I wanted to. I read the important bits to Ellie, who clearly didn't know whether to be shocked or amused, and then I put it back in the chest. Since it was perfectly obvious Lord Robert didn't deserve me, he could have his pearls back and tell his conniving mother it had all gone wrong!

But still, no yellow powder anywhere.

Ellie had found one pillowslip that didn't belong there and put it in her bag. Then she looked at me. "Well?" she said.

"I'm still going to help him get out of the Fleet," I told her. "But I certainly won't marry him. Now, Lady Sarah next, I think."

Ellie raised her eyebrows. "Why her?" she asked curiously.

"Lady Sarah was after Sir Gerald at the ball," I explained. "Maybe she hated him because he was chasing me." Then I added bitterly, "Though I know for a fact he was only doing what his uncle, Lord Worthy, told him. After my inheritance too, no doubt."

"Well, of course he was," said Ellie tartly. "They all were, except Sir Charles, who is surely rich enough."

We came out of Lord Robert's chamber and Ellie thanked the man, who went on playing with his cards. We walked on quickly down the Stone Gallery, across the little bridge, and into the upper story of the Privy Gallery to the chambers of the Maids of Honour and Ladies-in-Waiting.

In my chamber, Ellie sorted through the many pots and potions belonging to Lady Sarah. Not one of them was sulphur-yellow, though several were purple and more than one looked and smelled like dung. There were the usual white lead and cinnabar to make a red colour, and ground lapis lazuli and malachite for colouring eyelids blue or green, and some sticks of kohl. One bottle held something which Ellie sniffed and announced was probably a tincture of tansy and pennyroyal mint, and another was labelled FOR THE ALLUREMENT OF ALL KINDS OF LOVE, which made me laugh.

There was also a miniature of Sarah, which made her face much more heart-shaped than it really is and her chest even bigger. We also found dozens and dozens of love letters from moonstruck courtiers, including several each from Sir Charles, Lord Robert, and Sir Gerald! I scowled. They were supposed to be courting me; how dare they write rubbish to Lady Sarah, too? Surely having a big chest isn't *that* important?

"Yes, it is," said Ellie, when I put this to her.

I couldn't resist poking my nose round the door of Mrs. Champernowne's chamber, which was tidy and clean, with a big pile of books next to the bed, including two with nothing except boring sermons in them. No yellow powder.

We decided to look in Lord Worthy's chambers as well—it was only fair to search everyone's room. There was more paper piled up there than I have ever seen in my life. Ellie poked around, found a sheet with a nasty stain on it under the bed, and put it in her bag. I discovered a recipe to cure baldness together with a screw of green powder and several pots of ointment. I took the lid off one of the pots, but it smelled so strongly of horse dung that Ellie screwed up her face in disgust—though she was on the other side of the room—and I was nearly overcome! I quickly put the lid back on.

Then off we went to look at Sir Charles's room. Ellie protested at this. "Sir Charles is a kind old thing. He left me a lovely gift on Christmas day with two mince pies—and he made sure I got them," she said, with her hands on her hips.

"Well, we've got to investigate everybody who's even vaguely possible, Ellie—nobody's beyond suspicion except the Queen," I said firmly.

Sir Charles's Grace-and-Favour Chamber was near to the Court Gate, close to one of the small staging stables.

There was a servant there, fast asleep on the truckle bed, so Ellie and I had to creep about. We did have the excuse of looking for Mrs. Twynhoe's pillowslips. We checked the few pots on the table, looked under the bed and in the clothes chest. No yellow powder.

It wasn't until we were about to go out of the door again that I realized a funny thing about Sir Charles's shoes. They were lined up at the foot of the bed—two pairs of smart shoes to wear at Court, one pair of riding boots, all quite new. And then there were other pairs of shoes under the bed, and another pair of riding boots, rather more worn. But these looked smaller, and when I put one of the old shoes next to one of the new ones, I could see clearly that the old ones were quite a lot smaller. "Look at that," I whispered to Ellie. "Isn't it odd?"

"What?" said Ellie.

"His shoes. Look, the new ones are big and the old ones under the bed are small. It's as if Sir Charles's feet grew suddenly, like mine did last year. But he's too old to have growing feet."

Ellie looked and frowned in puzzlement.

Suddenly I heard footsteps in the passage. Sir Charles's voice called out, "Stevens, are you there?"

Ellie and I looked at each other in horror, and then Ellie scuttled under the bed and I went with her. We hid in a nest of footwear and old hose as Sir Charles came into the room.

I looked at his feet. He had another pair of boots on, very smart, brand new, and his feet were very big. I tried to remember Sir Charles's feet when I'd seen them before. Had they changed?

Sir Charles went over to the manservant on the truckle bed and shook him awake.

"Wuzzat?" muttered the man. Then he woke up properly and we heard him scrambling to his feet. "Um. Yes, Mr. Amesbury."

Ellie and I looked at each other. *Mr.* Amesbury?

"Go and check on my brother. Make sure he has water and can't get out," said the man who I had thought was Sir Charles.

"Yes, sir, if you say so," replied Stevens sullenly.

"I do say so, Stevens." The voice was cold and nasty, nothing like Sir Charles's friendly rumble.

I felt my jaw dropping open. Sir Charles wasn't Sir Charles—he was somebody else entirely! With the same face, maybe, but bigger feet and . . . A thought popped into my head. Didn't Sir Charles have a brother? I screwed up my eyes, trying to remember. A brother who had died in France . . .

If he'd died! What was his name? Harry? No. Hector.

"Best put a knife in him, sir, then drop him in the Thames," said Stevens, who was pulling on his jerkin. "That way—"

"Thank you for your advice, Stevens. I am perfectly well aware of what's best," snapped the impostor. "However, I cannot possibly do it until I know all his business dealings—and where he has hidden the deeds to his house."

"Don't think he'll tell you, sir," said Stevens. "Not wivout some better persuading."

"I know my brother, Stevens. He'll tell eventually rather than starve."

What a horrible way to talk about your brother! Ellie's eyes were like saucers. I was having to hold my hand over my mouth because the smell of stale cheese from the old hose was making me want to cough.

"And then once I'm safe I think I shall become ill for a while, so I can get rid of this padding," the impostor continued. He clearly was the not-so-Honourable Hector Amesbury, brother to Sir Charles.

Hector sat on his bed and changed into his riding boots with help from Stevens.

"First I must make an appearance at the stables," he said, "or somebody will wonder why my horse-mad fool of a brother has suddenly gone off the beasts. But then I shall come and . . . talk . . . to him again. Tell him that."

"Yes, sir." Stevens was by the door. "Couldn't I just . . . rough him up a bit—give him a taster, sir?"

"Very well. But don't do too much damage," Hector told him, still in that nasty cold voice.

"No, sir."

I still had my hand over my mouth, fighting not to cough. I really hoped Hector would go soon so I could get away from the hose. Ellie didn't seem to mind the smell but she was shaking. What kind of brother was Hector Amesbury? He'd imprisoned Sir Charles and was starving him! It was outrageous. Especially as Sir Charles was so fond of his food.

As the door shut behind them I scrambled out as quick as I could. Ellie followed more slowly, still trembling.

"Lord save us!" I said. "Perhaps *he* murdered Sir Gerald."

"He must have done! If he could imprison and starve his own brother . . ." Ellie shook her head. "And poor Sir Charles loving his food, and all."

"Exactly," I agreed. "And that's why Doucette didn't like him," I added thoughtfully. "Doucette *knew* it wasn't Sir Charles, the clever animal. And that's why he couldn't sing 'Greensleeves' properly at the ball! But why? Why would anybody do this to their own brother?"

We rushed back up to the Long Gallery to tell Masou. He was carefully flipping himself over from walking on his hands to standing upright, doing a somersault on the way.

He soon stopped as he listened to our story, though.

"We have to rescue Sir Charles," I said firmly. The other two just gawped at me.

"How?" demanded Ellie.

"It's obvious—we have to find out where he is and go there to free him," I told her. "Somebody has to follow Hector Amesbury and find out where he goes."

Masou looked at the two of us, then looked theatrically round the room, and then put his finger to his own chest.

I smiled sweetly at him and nodded.

Masou started putting on his shoes and pattens and clopped to the door of the gallery.

"He should be at the stables now," I said. "He said he'd go and see his brother afterwards."

Masou nodded and ran down the stairs. Then he ran back up again to ask, "What if he takes a boat?"

I felt in my petticoat and found some pennies, which I tossed to Masou. "If he catches you, pretend that you were about to ask him for a job," I suggested. Masou grinned, then went back downstairs again.

Ellie and I went back to Sir Charles's chamber and searched it more thoroughly, starting at one corner and going all the way round to the other. Nothing. Not the faintest smallest smidgeon of powder of any colour, let alone yellow, nor any staining. So Ellie took a couple of dirty shirts and we went back to Mrs. Bea, who received the pillowslips and shirts, checked them, and told Ellie to take them all down to the laundry and get back to work.

Then Mrs. Bea looked shrewdly at me. "Did you find anything interesting?" she asked.

For a moment I wanted to tell her all about Sir Charles and Hector, but there was a risk she might tell Mrs. Champernowne and then where would we be? So I shook my head and tried not to look as excited as I felt.

"No darkwort anywhere." I tried to look disappointed and I think I managed it quite well.

"Hmph. Come back to me tomorrow, my dear, and I shall tell you if any apothecaries have sold it recently—they may not remember, mind, or they might have been paid to keep quiet. But I'll ask for you. It would be a sad thing if Lord Robert were to lose his head over this."

"Wouldn't he hang?" asked Ellie ghoulishly, still hovering at the doorway. She hated to miss out on any gossip. "I thought that's what happened to murderers."

"That's right, Ellie, but being a nobleman, he can ask for the mercy of an axe," Mrs. Bea explained.

It didn't sound like much of a mercy to me. But still it was nice of her to help us and I said so. That made her laugh a lot, which made her pink face quite wobbly.

"Lord above, Lady Grace," she said, "I don't want anyone who owes me money to be executed."

"Does he owe you money, too?" I asked.

"Certainly," she replied. "For three wart-charmings and a spell against tongue-tie. And a spell to enchant cards in his favour, but I only get that if it works, and I don't suppose it has."

I scowled. "He owes everybody money—that's why he wanted to marry me."

"Of course he did, dear—you didn't think he loved you, did you? Did you love him?"

"Certainly not," I said, tossing my head. "He hasn't exactly done anything very lovable for me and he hasn't a word to say for himself. Besides, it's undignified to fall in love; that's for men to do."

Mrs. Bea chuckled. "Quite right. A well-born lady like you has no business falling in love and I'm glad to hear you've got your head well sewn on."

"Unlike Lord Robert," put in Ellie, and snickered.

I gave Mrs. Bea back her cap and apron and went

to my chamber to find that my dinner had been left outside the door for me. There was manchet bread, salt beef and potherbs, and a hard cheese with pickled eringo root against the scurvy. I gobbled it all down and I have been scribbling away at my daybooke ever since, but now someone is coming.

Midday

God's bones! There's so much to tell. I hardly know where to start and I'm so tired from being up all night again. But I must write this down no matter how much my head is whirling because otherwise I won't sleep at all. And besides, this was a most wondrous midnight adventure!

Last time I was interrupted it was Mrs. Champernowne bustling in.

"Wherever did you go, child?" she wanted to know. "The Queen was asking for you."

"I . . . went for a walk," I said, hoping it didn't sound as silly to her as it did to me, "around the palace. The Queen did say I could—"

"I think you have been treated very gently, Lady Grace," said Mrs. Champernowne severely. "There had better be no more trouble from you. Now get your kirtle on and attend Her Majesty at supper."

Lord Worthy was dining with the Queen again but this time I wasn't invited. I just brought the Queen's wine when she beckoned me and held a napkin for her to dry her fingers after she rinsed them. The Queen was quite distant to me, and I was desperate to let her know what I'd discovered. I wondered how Masou was getting on. Was he back yet? Was he safe? I chewed a fingernail nervously, and Her Majesty told me off.

The tumblers came in and, thank the Lord, Masou was among them, walking in on his hands and backwards somersaulting onto his feet. He stared at me and winked, so I could hardly wait until I had an excuse to leave the Queen's side. At last I had to go down to the buttery to refill a pitcher with ale. The jugglers and tumblers were there, drinking thirstily. Masou made a great flourish of taking the pitcher and filling it at the barrel for me. Then we went into a little alcove and Masou told me the story.

"I followed Sir Charles . . . ," Masou said, and mimed tiptoeing after him, dodging from tree to tree.

"It's really his brother Hector," I corrected him.

Masou rolled his eyes. "Who is telling this story?" he demanded. I smiled and gestured to him and he made an elaborate bow. "So I followed the Evil Brother to the Palace of Horses, praying to Allah that he would not take a horse to visit the Unfortunate One. Allah be praised, he did not. He scowled about at the grooms for a while and then went down to the watersteps and shouted, 'Oars!' A black ship with black sails, rowed by a green serpent, came. He stepped aboard and the snake rowed him away towards London town.

"After the black ship had departed, I shouted, too, and lo! a golden barque with a ruby sail appeared, rowed by a yellow serpent, who said, 'What is your desire, O Prince of Acrobats?' I jumped aboard and beseeched the serpent to follow the Evil Brother's boat, at which he transformed to an ugly djinni and said, 'Then pay sixpence for it.' Alas, nothing would do but that I must pay, and so he rowed and followed the Evil Brother to some steps which shone with silver and gold and led to a fair garden and little stone houses. Here I paid the djinni and crept ashore. I hid in a wondrous bush that covered me like a Cloak of Invisibility while the Evil Brother went to one of the houses and knocked on the door. It was opened by another evil one, with blood on his knuckles. I did not see the Unfortunate One but he was there, for so I heard Evil Brother say. And then, in great fear lest he find me, I went back down the steps and looked for a boat. At last I came across a little cockleshell with a cobweb sail steered by a monkey, who took me aboard when I begged him. And so I came back unto the Court just in time to tumble for the Queen."

Masou swept another bow and then stood with his arms folded looking very stern. I clapped. "What a wonderful story!" I said. "Is any of it true?"

"Certainly, in essence," said Masou, grinning. "I think the Unfortunate One is imprisoned in one of the little cottages of St. Mary Rounceval churchyard."

"We will have to go there tonight," I decided. My heart was sinking at what the Queen might say, but what else could we do? "Is there any way we could get in without the guard knowing?"

Masou thought hard. "There are windows—I think they are glass, quite small, but I think I could pass. Yes, it can be done. But, my lady, it would be very dangerous—"

"Then we'll do it," I said. "Can you arrange for a boat?"

Masou bowed with his two hands crossed on his

chest. "I am my lady's to command," he said, and cartwheeled away.

I hurried back to the Withdrawing Room with the pitcher and then put my hand to my head and curtsied to the Queen, explaining in front of everyone that I had a megrim from the excitement of the last few days and asking if I could go to my bed.

Her Majesty didn't quite believe me, I could see that, but she let me go.

Once again I had to wait, lying stiff as a board with fright and excitement with a smock over my hunting kirtle, until Mary and Lady Sarah were back from attending the Queen—except Mary came back but there was no sign of Lady Sarah at all. Oh, well, I thought, I can tell on her if she tells on me.

I crept out while Mary snored, and tiptoed down the passageway to the Orchard door, where Masou and Ellie were waiting.

"Did you bring money?" asked Masou. "We must pay for the boat."

I had a few pennies. We threaded through the palace, dodging serving men and night-wandering courtiers, to the watersteps. Masou whistled softly, and a boat rowed close. It wasn't a normal Thames wherry; it was tiny, with a little sail and a scrawny boy about Masou's age rowing it.

"Who's he?" I hissed. "Is that the monkey in the cockleshell?"

"My lady, may I present my friend Kersey," said Masou with a flourish. "Kersey, this is the Lady Grace I told you about."

"What did you tell him?" I whispered.

Masou shrugged innocently.

The boy in the boat drew the oars in, snatched off his greasy cap, and made a bow. "Honoured, lady," he said. "Sorry I din't believe you, Masou. Come aboard, ladies," he added, winking at Ellie.

Ellie sniffed. "Don't you go calling me a lady," she said sternly as she hopped in and I followed. "I'm here for to attend on my lady and save her reputation."

Masou elbowed me, and I pulled out my purse and gave Kersey all my pennies. He grunted and put them away in his sleeve, then coughed and looked embarrassed. "See, lady, Masou told me you was one of the Queen's Ladies-in-Waiting . . ."

"I'm a Maid of Honour," I said, wishing Masou could have kept his mouth shut.

"Right, Maid of Honour, and wot he said is that you get to see the Queen every day and she speaks to you."

"Yes, that's true," I admitted.

"I met the Queen once," Kersey said. "She was wearing all silver and black velvet and with diamonds in her hair and I held the boat for her when she went on her barge—'cos me dad's one of the relief bargemen—and squashed me thumb and she gave me her kerchief to bind it up and said she hoped as it would be better soon. She's wonderful, isn't she? Just gave me her own kerchief and said—"

"She's very kind to people who look after her," I agreed.

Kersey was rowing us along the northern bank of the Thames, dodging some of the dangerous eddies. He seemed more interested in talking than rowing, though, which worried me. "I wish I could see her every day like you." His face was shining with adoration. "How do you get to be a courtier?" he asked.

"Well, you have to be rich, or rich enough to pretend to be rich," I replied.

Kersey nodded. "How rich is that?"

"A velvet suit costs a hundred pounds, for a cheap one," I told him. He gasped, and shut up.

Masou tapped the side of the boat and Kersey rowed it close up to the shining, slimy wall of some houses near the water's edge. There was a row of windows overlooking the water, and watersteps going up to a gate.

"That is the cottage where Sir Charles is being held," whispered Masou, pointing to a house at the far end of the row. "There's a man guarding the door, so I will have to break in at the back."

Kersey was tying his craft up tight to the wall by a ring.

"I want to get up to that ledge there," said Masou, gesturing towards the windows. "And I need a diamond ring."

"Why?" asked Ellie.

Masou grinned, with a flash of white teeth. "For the reason that only diamond is of enough hardness to cut glass," he explained.

"Hmph," said Ellie.

There were diamonds in the pearl ring my mother gave me. I hesitated and then gave it to Masou.

He smiled at me because I could have said no, it was too valuable. "Now, it's fine that you are tall," he said to me. "But I hope you are strong, too. You must give me a lift up."

"Standing on the boat?" I asked.

"Yes. I could not use a ladder—too rigid," Masou explained.

Kersey was tying the other end of the boat to another ring.

"But—" I began.

"Kersey and Ellie will hold you steady. All you need do is stand firm and I shall climb you like a living tree."

Firm? On a boat? I saw a bit of stone sticking out and I leaned over and grabbed it.

"Good," Masou said, and sprang onto my back. He is quite small and very lithe, but he is also heavy. I went "Ooof!" and nearly fell down.

"I told you it should be me," sniffed Ellie. "I'm stronger."

"But not tall enough," said Masou, fitting one foot onto my shoulder. "There, it's just enough."

The boat creaked and tilted sideways. Masou climbed on my other shoulder and balanced. It hurt! My shoulders felt like they would break; there was a sort of bounce and then the weight was off.

Masou was crouched on the ledge, peering through the window. He muttered in disappointment, reached round a piece of wall, and slid onto the next windowsill. Another grunt. Ellie and I were staring at him, really scared that all the adventure was for nothing. I noticed that Masou had something long wrapped in cloth and slung across his back, and I wondered what it was.

He slid along and reached for the next window, peered through, and said, "Hah! Allah be praised."

He crouched there for what seemed a long time and there was a dreadful scraping screeching noise, which must have been the diamond cutting glass, then a tapping. A big piece of window came out, held by Masou with his fingers and a knife, and he threw it down into the Thames. Then he reached in, found a latch, and opened the window. He uncoiled a rope from round his waist and tied one end to the window post. "Climb up by the rope now, Lady Grace," he called softly down to me.

I wasn't sure how to do it, but Masou told me to wrap it round my waist and pull myself up by my arms, putting my toes into the cracks in the wall. It was very slimy and slippery. I nearly went in the water twice, but I managed to get up on the ledge and crouch there, my heart going *bam-da-da-bam!* like a drum at a dance.

Masou moved the rope so it hung into the room, then dropped down. I followed. There was soft straw, a dreadful smell of damp, an unemptied chamberpot, and a rather fat man lying huddled up in a cloak in the corner.

I went over to him and touched him on the shoulder. He snorted, and jumped awake with his fists up. I backed into the corner.

"Who? What?" he shouted angrily.

"Sir Charles?" I asked, because I wasn't sure. Masou was busy with a tinder box. He lit a candle and then I saw it definitely was Sir Charles, though he looked terrible. His beard was untrimmed and his hair was standing on end. He was in his shirt-sleeves with the cloak wrapped around him and he had a nasty black eye as well.

"Good heavens, Lady Grace, what in the name of God . . . ?" His eyes narrowed with suspicion. "Did my brother bring you?"

"No." I scowled at that. "I don't know what sort of brother he is, but *we've* come to rescue you."

I practically gabbled as I told him what we'd found out and how we came to help, and he shook his head as if bewildered. Meanwhile, Masou had unslung the thing on his back and was unwrapping it.

Masou bowed. "Sir, I think the window is too small for you, but I brought this." He handed Sir Charles the long poignard dagger he had brought with him.

Sir Charles gripped the hilt, tested the blade, then

shook his head. "I can't leave. Look." He lifted one of his feet and we saw there was a manacle round his ankle and a short chain stapled to the wall.

Masou smiled again and brought out a little wallet which had hooks and files in it. He checked the ring around Sir Charles's ankle while I listened at the locked door to make sure the man guarding it hadn't heard anything. There was a series of scraping noises and then a brisk sound of filing. At last I heard a click, and next moment Sir Charles was standing up with the poignard in his hand. Even though he was a fat old man, he looked very angry and quite frightening. "Pray, now, climb back out of the window," he ordered.

"But, Sir Charles, we can help you . . . ," I began.

"Lady Grace, this is not a sight for you. I will meet you at the watersteps," he replied firmly.

Masou bowed to Sir Charles and held the rope for me to climb up, which was even more difficult the second time because my hands were so sore.

We dropped back into the boat and waited.

Suddenly we heard banging and screaming from Sir Charles. "Help! Help! I'm choking . . . arghh . . ."

It didn't sound very realistic but there was the sound of a door being unlocked and then Stevens's voice. "Didn't you learn your lesson the first time, you—"

There was a thud, a scuffle, a horrible sort of crunching noise, a short cry—and then silence. A few minutes later we could hear Sir Charles breathing hard on the watersteps and see his broad silhouette there.

He got down carefully into the boat, which was distinctly overloaded with all of us, and washed the poignard and his hands in the water. Then he offered the blade back to Masou, who shook his head. Nobody said anything. In truth, I felt a bit sick.

Kersey rowed us all slowly and carefully back upriver to Whitehall, which took longer because the current was against him.

"What happened to you, Sir Charles?" I asked, so I wouldn't think about my queasy stomach and how close the water was as we struggled slowly upstream.

Sir Charles turned to me. "My lady, all I know is that I went for a nap after our ride on the day of the St. Valentine's Feast and woke up in that foul place with a chain on my leg," he said. "I could scarce believe it possible, and yet my twin brother was there, demanding to know where my papers were and what my business dealings were at the Royal Exchange." Sir Charles wiped his brow—he was sweating heavily, even though there was a chill in the air. "My twin brother, Hector, always hated me—even though I gave him money whenever he asked for it—I thought he was in France fighting the Papists. And then I had word that he was dead, as I told you. But there he was, threatening me with starvation and worse if I did not do as he demanded. Of course, I did not, as I *knew* I would then be a dead man for certain. But then he sent his henchman to threaten me and strike me—"

"What happened to Stevens?" I asked.

Sir Charles looked away. "Honour is satisfied for the blows he gave me. He is dead."

"Oh." That was all I could manage to say. It was hard to imagine plump, jolly Sir Charles, who took me riding and sang "Greensleeves" for me, killing someone with his own hands. Even with good reason.

"Good," said Ellie. "Serves 'im right."

I looked at the sky and saw it was nearly dawn. My heart went into my boots. We'd rescued Sir Charles but, oh, I was going to be in so much trouble.

Sir Charles saw my face and said very kindly,

"Never fear, Lady Grace, Her Majesty will be delighted with you presently. Let me but speak to her and she shall be reconciled." Then his face went back to being rather bleak.

Nobody said anything more as we struggled back up to Whitehall, with all of us paddling eventually against the tide. We reached the steps and climbed up them to find a bemused Yeoman of the Guard barring our path.

Kersey let us off and then rowed away to the kitchen steps as fast as he could.

I recognized the Yeoman, who sometimes guarded the Queen. "Good morning, Mitchell," I said. "Will you send to Her Majesty to say that I have rescued the real Sir Charles Amesbury from imprisonment by his brother and brought him back to her?" I did my best to sound as imperious and commanding as the Queen, though I fear my stained, green-wool, third-best kirtle did not help.

That put the cat among the pigeons! What a lot of fuss and flurrying around, while Her Majesty was awoken and prepared for an audience. Eventually we were all brought into the Presence Chamber, where the Queen was sitting on her throne looking absolutely furious, Lord Worthy at her side. Mary Shelton and Lady Sarah were peeping round the side of the dais, faces alight with curiosity. They must have come in to arrange the Queen's train and then managed not to be dismissed by pretending to be very intent on their embroidery.

The Queen didn't even look at me. I just hoped her fury was for the benefit of appearances. If she had truly tired of my adventures, I really was in trouble! Sir Charles stepped forwards, kneeled, and told her what he had told us on the boat. The Queen listened silently. Then, without comment, she sent for the man calling himself Sir Charles.

Hector Amesbury arrived, looking nervous. Sir Charles stood to face him, his hand on the poignard. At first glance, they were like two peas in a pod, save for Sir Charles being half-dressed and unshaven. But side by side I could see that Hector was an inch or so taller.

"I see my poor mad brother Hector Amesbury has escaped," sneered the pretend Sir Charles. "The poor fellow believes that he is really me. He's very convincing, I grant you."

"How could you do this, Hector?" said the real Sir Charles, sounding very sad. "I gave you a good income, I helped you to go to France—how could you do it?"

Hector shrugged. "His insanity is flamboyant, as

you see, Your Majesty. It is not surprising that your innocent Maid of Honour, Lady Grace, has been fooled by it."

The Queen looked from the real Sir Charles to the false one and back, then frowned. "How shall this be resolved, gentlemen?" she asked.

I was too excited to remember to kneel. I just burst out with: "Your Majesty, I know a way!"

After I'd said that there was a nasty silence.

"Well?" the Queen enquired. She didn't sound at all encouraging.

I swallowed and curtsied again. "We could ask one of Sir Charles's best friends," I said. "Doucette!"

And so we all went in a very odd sort of procession to the loose box where Doucette was stabled. Sir Charles smiled for the first time as he heard Doucette nicker.

"Here, horsey," said Hector Amesbury, looking scared. "Here!"

Doucette was led out of her loose box by one of the stableboys. As she approached Hector, she looked sulky, her head down. Then her head came up when she smelled Sir Charles and she whickered happily. She dragged her stableboy straight over to the real Sir Charles, who patted her neck and let her nuzzle him. For the first time his battered face relaxed and he looked like the jolly person I knew.

"See?" I said. "Have you ever known any horse that didn't love Sir Charles?"

Hector advanced on Doucette, looking very tense. "Now then, horsey, you know me," he said sternly, reaching for her bridle.

Doucette turned her head, put her ears back, made a disapproving snort, and nipped his arm where he'd stuck it out towards her.

He jerked it back, looked desperately from the horse to his brother to the Queen. By now everybody was scowling at him.

That was when he realized he was as good as dead. Suddenly he punched the man standing next to him and started running for the Court Gate.

Two of the Queen's Guard went after him and one made a huge flying leap onto his back, while the other grabbed his doublet and swung him down. He went over, yelling that it wasn't fair, in a pile of crimson velvet and fists, and all the padding came out of his doublet.

The guards brought him back to where the Queen was standing, with Sir Charles by her side. She stared at Hector with her eyes like chips of ice and her lips so tight they had almost disappeared. She looked terrifying.

"Mr. Amesbury, you have one minute to avoid a trial for high treason by confessing everything." Her voice was like ice, too.

Hector had lost his nerve. He fell to his knees and put his face in his hands. "It's not my fault—you can't blame me for trying to do something to better my life, when that maggot stole my rightful inheritance. He struts around claiming to be the elder but it's me: *I'm* the elder twin, *I* should have inherited the estates and lived in luxury while he should have gone to France to fight for starveling Huguenots!"

Since half the stableboys and dog-pages in the place were leaning out of loose boxes and windows to eavesdrop on this, the Queen announced that we would return to her Presence Chamber and so back we all processed, Hector surrounded by the Queen's Guard and Sir Charles gallantly offering the Queen his arm—which she politely refused. (I don't blame her. A most unpleasant smell surrounded Sir Charles due to his having been imprisoned for days.)

In the Presence Chamber, Masou, Ellie, and I all sat by the wall while the Queen sent for a clerk to take everything down, and my uncle, Dr. Cavendish. Mary Shelton and Lady Sarah had picked up their embroidery again and were sitting quietly in the corner, hoping the Queen wouldn't notice them and send them away.

Sir Charles stood and told of his and Hector's dramatic birth, so long ago it was before the Queen was born! There had been twin sons born to the Amesbury household and a scarlet thread was tied about the wrist of the first-born twin. But it was the depths of winter and Mother Corbett, the midwife, had built up the fire in the lying-in chamber.

"Alas, some swaddling bands, hung before the fire to warm, caught alight," said Sir Charles. "In seconds the whole lying-in chamber, with all the hangings, was roaring with flame. My father ran in and carried my mother out. The midwife caught up the babies and saved them. All the men from the village came up to make a bucket-chain and out the flames, and at last the fire was stopped, though that part of the house was almost destroyed. But in all the confusion the scarlet thread upon my wrist was lost. Only Mother Corbett said I was the elder twin because she remembered carrying the first-born on her right arm and the younger one on her left."

Hector snorted. "The word of a drunken old witch . . ."

"She remembered clearly and never wavered—" began Sir Charles.

"How dare you!" shrieked Hector, who seemed to have taken all leave of his senses. "It was *I* who was the elder twin and *you* the pretender. I have known it ever since old Mother Corbett told me the tale when I was nine. I have known it and you have always denied it."

"I deny it because it is not true," said Sir Charles levelly.

"And so," said the Queen, "what did you do to right what you conceived as an injustice, Mr. Amesbury?"

Hector looked at the rush matting, his face working, and I noticed that there was spittle on his chin. "I was near enough blown to pieces on a French battlefield," he said. "I took my survival as a sign. Wherefore should I struggle through war and bloodshed when my rightful inheritance waited in England? I had my commander write to my brother to say I was dead, and then I returned, in secrecy, to England." He looked up, his broad Charles-ish face sour and ugly with spite. "Sir Charles's pageboy took a shilling to put laudanum in his wine and I smuggled him unconscious out of the Court in one of the carts bringing hay for the horses. I had already rented the abandoned cottages at St. Mary Rounceval. I took my brother's place—I only needed to have new footwear made that fitted me, and wear his clothes with a little padding stuffed inside. And so I fooled everyone."

He laughed and wagged a finger. "You were all so blind, it was almost laughable. All you see are the clothes. I decided I must marry the Cavendish girl to secure a fortune of my own. And to do it, I first needed to—"

"Kill Sir Gerald?" asked the Queen flintily.

"Yes," Hector agreed enthusiastically. "And likewise be sure that Lord Robert was accused of the murder, so I would be the last suitor and could be sure of marrying the girl. That way, no matter if someone discovered my true identity, I would still be her husband and still have her estates."

He laughed more loudly, sounding slightly hysterical now. "I fooled you all again with my genius and cunning! I simply went to Lord Robert's chamber and cut an aiglet from one of his doublets; then I hurried to Sir Gerald's chamber, where I found him so sottish with drink that he made no stir when I crept in.

And so I took the dagger that lay on the chest, stabbed it into Sir Gerald's back where he lay, and left Lord Robert's aiglet on the pillow. Thus I rid myself of all competition at a single stroke!"

"And then you came back to the Banqueting House to dance and feign kindness to Lord Robert?" demanded the Queen.

Hector nodded, looking very proud of himself.

"Was it so light a thing for you then, to kill a man who was helpless?" The Queen's voice was soft but cut like steel.

Hector shrugged.

"But Hector, for God's sake," broke in Sir Charles. "Why in God's name did you think such a mad plan would work?"

"Of course it would have worked. Why shouldn't it? Nobody would suspect dear old Charles Amesbury of killing Sir Gerald—he's got plenty of enemies, especially Lord Robert. . . . And once I was married to the Cavendish heiress, none of that would have mattered anyway. I would have been safe—rich like you. No more struggling to find a living, no more fighting in France . . ." Hector seemed to have forgotten completely that there were other people listening, especially the Queen. He pointed his finger at me. "Nothing went wrong until that interfering girl poked her nose in where it wasn't wanted."

I sniffed. I dare say he would have called anyone who found him out "interfering."

"*Lady* Grace," Sir Charles said severely to Hector, "was good enough to rescue me from the vile dungeon you put me in."

"Well, Lord Robert should think twice about marrying some girl who might take it into her head to run off one night and rescue somebody!"

The Queen's eyebrows went right up her forehead at this. Hector saw her and stopped talking, his face twitching.

After a long and impressive silence, the Queen spoke. "Mr. Hector Amesbury, you shall be committed to the Fleet, and of course my Lord Robert shall be released. We shall then see to it that you are arraigned for the murder of Sir Gerald Worthy—"

I coughed. I had to. You're not supposed to interrupt the Queen.

She looked in my direction and sighed. "Yes, Lady Grace. What have you to add?" she asked.

I stood up, wishing that I didn't have big stains all over my poor hunting kirtle. I had to say it, though, because somebody who has once killed with poison might do it again . . . and again.

"Well, you see, Your Majesty, I don't think Hector Amesbury *did* kill Sir Gerald, even if he thought he did. He was so anxious to get rid of him, he didn't realize that Sir Gerald was already dead."

"*What?*" exclaimed Hector, whose eyes looked as though they might pop out of his head.

"What are you talking about, Grace?" the Queen enquired patiently.

"Someone had been there before, Your Majesty. You see, my uncle, Dr. Cavendish, noticed that the wound in Sir Gerald's back hadn't bled, and he deduced that this must be because Sir Gerald was already dead when he was stabbed," I explained.

My uncle threw me a grateful look.

"And then, when I . . . um . . . when I went to visit Sir Gerald in the chapel, I noticed that he had a sulphur-yellow staining on his lips and there was a nasty bitter smell."

The Queen's expression hardened. Clearly, she knew what I was talking about. "Darkwort," she said grimly.

"Yes, Your Majesty," said Dr. Cavendish, sounding dolefully hung over again, "I'm afraid so. It is my intention to obtain a Court order to open the body. I suspect we shall find that the liver is quite blackened."

Lord Worthy went grey at this talk of opening his nephew's body. I felt quite sorry for him. Looking pale and drawn, he leaned forward to speak to the Queen. "Your Majesty," he said, hoarsely, "I find myself rather overcome. Would you be so good as to allow me to withdraw?"

The Queen looked at him with concern. "Of course, my Lord Worthy," she replied kindly. "Do you require the services of Dr. Cavendish?"

"No, no, not at all," Lord Worthy said hurriedly. "Dr. Cavendish is needed here. A brief rest and I am sure I shall be quite recovered." He hurried from the Presence Chamber and the Queen turned back to the doctor.

"So when Mr. Amesbury stabbed Sir Gerald, he was stabbing a corpse!" she declared.

Hector was giggling like a small child. "That's not murder, is it? Tell her, Charles!" he pleaded, and Charles shook his head. "You can't hang me for stabbing a corpse, can you?" Hector pursued.

"It was attempted murder," said the Queen coldly, "and shall be tried as such. You shall also be tried for kidnapping and false imprisonment of your own brother, and the *wicked* imposture you attempted on ourselves. And if the jury does not decide you should hang, then I should think it's likely you shall spend the rest of your days in Bedlam, since it seems you are quite mad."

Her Majesty signalled for Hector Amesbury to be taken away. He went, still giggling and shaking his head, seeming to have retreated into his own world.

"Sir Charles, I am pleased that Dr. Cavendish has declared you not to have taken any great hurt from your brother's wicked practices."

Turning even ruddier than usual, Sir Charles went nearer and bent onto one knee. "Your Majesty, you are too kind," he puffed. His intention was clearly to kiss the Queen's hand. But Her Majesty hastily held a lace handkerchief to her nose and bade Sir Charles rise to go and take his rest, saying that of course he could remain in his Grace-and-Favour Chamber as long as he needed to.

After Sir Charles had left, the Queen looked serious again. "So we still have a poisoner abroad at Court," she said gravely.

I stepped forward. "Yes, I'm afraid so, Your Majesty. I knew that if news spread that a darkwort poisoning was suspected, the villain who had it would get rid of any remains. So I helped Ellie in her laundry round and we secretly searched all the chambers for darkwort. But we found none. It was while we were searching Sir Charles's chamber that we overheard Hector talking of how he had imprisoned his brother."

"I see," said Her Majesty. She nodded to Ellie, and then beckoned her and Masou forward.

They kneeled down in front of her.

Ellie was now as white as one of the sheets she helps to iron. I was surprised she was so overawed. I knew she had collected the Queen's dirty shifts for washing hundreds of times. But I suppose it's not the same as actually meeting the person who wears them.

Masou just went a bit grey. But he managed to flourish off his cap in quite a good bow.

"Masou got us downriver and did all the hard work of climbing up to the window and getting through it," I explained.

The Queen nodded graciously. "Oh, I recognize you," she said to Masou. "Will Somers thinks very highly of you—though he complains you are sometimes hard to find. And now we know why. . . ."

Masou looked rather sheepish, and I had to try not to laugh.

"Well, Ellie and Masou, you appear to be loyal and supportive friends to my Lady Grace," Her

Majesty observed. "Thank you. You may leave us now."

Both of them scurried out, looking very relieved. At least Masou remembered to back the last few steps, though Ellie tripped on her petticoat when she tried to copy him.

I guessed they would wait outside, trying to eavesdrop, if they weren't shooed away. They passed Mrs. Twynhoe on their way out.

"Is it urgent, Bea?" asked the Queen rather crossly.

Mrs. Bea curtsied and fanned herself. "I'm afraid it is, Your Majesty," she replied. "Lady Grace here told me of the dastardly doings with darkwort in Court. And I must tell you what I found."

"Ah . . . ," said the Queen. "This is very timely, Bea. We are all listening."

Mrs. Bea curtsied again. "Now then, I went myself about the apothecaries in Westminster and London town. I know 'em all, and most would talk only to those they know about their dealings with darkwort. Only one of 'em—my old contact in Cheapside—had sold darkwort in recent weeks."

"And did you find out the purchaser?" the Queen demanded grimly.

"Why, Your Majesty, that's why I had to hurry myself and tell you," Mrs. Bea replied. "Please believe me when I say I would never do nothing to hurt you, Your Grace, never in all the world."

"I know that, Bea," said the Queen softly, because Mrs. Bea looked very upset and was twisting her hands round about each other.

"Well, but . . . it's a terrible thing, Your Majesty," Mrs. Bea went on. "I couldn't believe it when I heard it. In fact, I told the man he was a liar, which annoyed him. . . ."

The Queen tapped her fingers on the arm of her chair of state and Mrs. Bea collected up her thoughts. "He told me that a skinny serving man bought the darkwort from him. He was wrapped up in a cloak. But when he took out his purse to pay, the cloak slipped open—enough for the apothecary to recognize the servant's livery. It was Lord Worthy's," Mrs. Bea finished dramatically.

There was a stunned silence.

The Queen broke it. "Impossible!" she shouted. "Besides," she added, "Lady Grace and that good wench Ellie searched all the Court chambers for evidence of darkwort—including Lord Worthy's—and found none."

"That's true, Mrs. Bea," I confirmed. "We found no yellow powder anywhere—"

At this, my Uncle Cavendish started. "But Grace," he said urgently, "darkwort powder . . . it is not yellow, my dear, it is green."

I stood there open-mouthed.

Mrs. Bea nodded vigorously at me. "Yes, my love—pure darkwort is green. It's the mixing with wine that turns it yellow and makes it stain such that not even ten-day-old urine will shift it."

Ellie and I *had* found green powder in Lord Worthy's chamber. And I had seen green staining on his cuff. Heart thudding, I told the Queen.

Her Majesty became as still as a statue, her face hard like marble. "Mr. Hatton!" she roared.

One of her Gentlemen put his head round a door. I caught a glimpse of Ellie on the other side, trying not to be noticed so she wouldn't get sent away and miss everything. I was sure now that Masou must be eavesdropping as well.

"Send for my Lord Worthy to come to the Presence Chamber at once!" the Queen commanded.

Mr. Hatton disappeared at a run. We stood awkwardly and waited—me, Mrs. Bea, and Uncle Cavendish. My hands were clenched and my mind was racing. Yes, it fitted . . . But why had he done it? Why would Lord Worthy want to poison Sir Gerald—his own nephew? It just didn't make sense.

At last Mr. Hatton returned and announced my Lord Worthy, who looked tired and strained.

"My lord," said the Queen formally, "I have it on good authority that one of your servants purchased darkwort recently. And that it was seen in your chamber."

Lord Worthy turned pale, his eyelids fluttering. For a moment he couldn't speak. Then he croaked, "Your Majesty?"

"Darkwort, my lord!" the Queen rapped out. "You deny it?"

"Of a certainty, I do, Your Majesty. It is out of all reason. How dare anyone put forth such foul lies . . . that I, Lord Worthy, should have dealings with such terrible poison . . . what villainous mischief . . ." By now Lord Worthy was gabbling.

"Your Majesty, may I ask Lord Worthy a question?" I put in hesitantly.

The Queen nodded.

Lord Worthy looked at me. "What? What are you doing here? This is no business for a Maid of Honour."

"She has made it her business, my lord," the Queen snapped, "and so have I!"

"My lord, I believe that you have a green stain that may be darkwort on your shirt-cuff. Would you please show us?" I asked nervously.

Lord Worthy's face became closed and haughty. He lifted both his hands. "By all means. See? There is no darkwort staining on my cuffs."

My heart sank. Lord Worthy must have changed into a clean shirt—the evidence was now lost in the wash.

Just then there was a timid knock on the door.

"What is it? We are busy!" the Queen bellowed.

Ellie sidled awkwardly into the room, curtsying and bobbing her head like a pigeon. "Ahem . . . ," she began. "I couldn't help overhearing, earlier . . . And I thought I should confess that, as I've been . . . otherwise occupied, as you might say . . . I'm run-nin' a bit behind on me laundry duties. . . ." With that, Ellie brought out from behind her back a rather grimy-looking man's shirt.

My heart leaped. "Is that whose I think it is, Ellie?" I asked. "My Lord Worthy's?"

Ellie nodded, with a respectful curtsy.

"This is preposterous!" burst out Lord Worthy.

"Am I to be accused by a maid and a servant?" But by now his complexion was almost grey.

"My lord, please be quiet," said the Queen in a very frightening voice.

The mood was extremely heavy. It even silenced the songbirds. None of them so much as peeped.

Still bobbing, Ellie came closer and held out the sleeves of the shirt for all to see.

One shirt-cuff was stained with green.

"Well, my lord?" the Queen demanded.

"Hmph . . . ," said Lord Worthy. "Spinach from yesterday's dinner."

Mrs. Bea shook her head solemnly. "I'd stake my life on that not being spinach," she said. She went to the table and brought the wine jug, then dripped a little onto the cuff. The red of the wine spread over the green—becoming edged with yellow as it did so.

"Darkwort, Your Majesty," she said firmly.

"Am I to be accused by a witch now?" Lord Worthy blustered. "Where is your sworn justice, Your Majesty?"

"Darkwort," my Uncle Cavendish confirmed. "No doubt about it."

"Have a care, my Lord Worthy," warned the Queen, standing up. "You have served me faithfully and I had thought you my friend." Her voice was rising. "Either you stop lying to me now—immediately!—and tell me exactly and truthfully what has happened, or I will put you in the Tower, by God, and have you examined by Mr. Rackmaster Norton. *Do you understand, my lord?*" The last words were at a full-throated roar.

Everyone winced at the thought of Rackmaster Norton.

Lord Worthy stared at her and then something seemed to melt or crumble inside him. He got down stiffly onto his knees and bowed his head. Into the silence we heard his voice whisper, "Yes. It is darkwort."

I couldn't breathe. Could he . . . ? Had he . . . ?

"Your own nephew, Lord Worthy?" said the Queen.

"No!" Lord Worthy exclaimed. "That was never the intention . . ." He sighed, then continued, his voice flat and dull. "The darkwort was intended for Lord Robert . . . and the blame for Sir Charles. . . .

"It was clear my Lady Grace favoured Lord Robert—and that she also made time for Sir Charles. But I could not possibly allow her to marry anyone except my nephew. So I put the darkwort into Lord

Robert's wine at the ball, and intended to put the remains of the powder amongst Sir Charles's belongings. All would have been well . . ." Lord Worthy put his face into his hands. "But then Gerald had to go and make a fool of himself at the ball, and you insisted he drink from Lord Robert's own cup. I was horrified, but how could I tell him to go against Your Majesty's orders?"

Lord Worthy laughed. A horrible, hollow, defeated sound. "Imagine my shock when the alarm was raised that poor Gerald had been *stabbed*, not poisoned—and moreover, that Lord Robert had done the deed!"

He turned his gaze on me, his eyes burning. "Of course, with a stabbing, rather than a poisoning, being recorded, I refrained from planting the remaining darkwort in Sir Charles's chamber. . . ."

Feeling very sad about the whole mess, I looked away.

"But Lord Worthy," said the Queen, "*why* was it so imperative that Lady Grace marry your nephew?"

"So that neither she, nor anyone else, would find out . . . ," Lord Worthy whispered brokenly.

"Find out what?" The Queen's tone of voice was steely and cold. I think she knew what was coming next, though I didn't.

"That Lady Grace has no estates, no fortune at all."

I felt as if somebody had stabbed me in the stomach. I couldn't even gasp. My guardian, Lord Worthy, was supposed to be my friend and my helper!

"Explain!" the Queen snapped.

"When I was appointed guardian to Lady Grace a year ago, I was in some debt," Lord Worthy began. "So I took the opportunity to mortgage Lady Grace's estate. But my financial situation grew worse rather than better. Within months, the moneylenders foreclosed and Lady Grace's estate was lost.

"It was unthinkable for either Lord Robert or Sir Charles to marry Lady Grace and discover this," Lord Worthy continued. "Only Gerald could be trusted not to disgrace me. . . ." He hung his head.

I felt sick and my stomach was whirling. Lord Worthy had stolen the inheritance my parents left me and then tried to get me to marry his nephew to cover it up? I could not believe it. Nor could Mary and Lady Sarah. They were staring at me, and Mary had tears of sympathy in her eyes. Suddenly their faces seemed to spin like a cartwheel in front of me. . . .

Mrs. Bea caught my arm. "Sit down, my dear."

I sat down with a bump on a cushion and she

pushed my head down. Some of the spinning in my stomach faded. Had I nearly fainted? How disgustingly like Lady Sarah! I gulped twice and sipped some of the wine Mrs. Bea brought me.

"Please, Your Majesty, I beg you, I had to do it, I couldn't let anyone find out, I—" Lord Worthy's voice had taken on a pathetic whining note.

"You *had* to try and poison my Lord Robert so you could hide your robbery from Lady Grace?" snapped the Queen. "You *had* to, my lord?"

"I . . ."

"You did not have to." The Queen shook her head. "You could have come to me when you first found yourself in financial difficulties, and I would have helped you. The money you needed could have come to you openly and honestly. There was no need of more murder in the Court."

"Please, Your Majesty . . ."

"Mr. Hatton, call the Gentlemen of the Guard. My Lord Worthy is to be committed to the Tower on charges of murder, corruption, falsehood, and endangering my life."

The Gentlemen of the Guard arrived and took Lord Worthy away, looking puzzled and frightened.

I was still sitting sideways on a cushion, waiting for my head to stop spinning.

Suddenly I started to cry, which was very embarrassing and I didn't want to, but I couldn't help it. It had all been such a shock.

Ellie came running over and put her arms round me. Mary Shelton was there, too, putting a clean handkerchief into my hand so I could blow my nose.

I thought of another awful thing and my stomach gave a swoop. "Your Grace, now I'm not rich any more, do I have to leave you?" I asked, feeling as if my heart would break again.

The Queen came to me in a rustle of damask and pulled me to her, crushing my cheek against a jewel on her bodice. "Of course not, Grace! You are my dearest god-daughter and Maid of Honour. You shall stay at Court as long as you like."

"Well then, at least you can marry your Lord Robert now," said Mrs. Bea in a sprightly there-there voice.

"I shall not," I sniffled. "He only wants my money. Besides, I've decided he's an idiot."

The Queen smiled. "I do believe I agree with you," she said.

That cheered me up so much that I kissed her on the cheek. "So I do not have to marry?"

"No, Grace, not for now," the Queen replied. "Though in due course, perhaps you will wish to. . . ."

In all the commotion, Masou had slipped into the room, too. "And if anyone does propose marriage to you now, it will surely be for love, not money," he said. "Mayhap it is a blessing that you are no longer rich, Lady Grace!"

"Precisely," said the Queen. "Well put, Masou."

She smiled at us all, and it's true what they say about the Queen, her smile *is* like magic. It makes you feel warm and safe.

She clasped my hand to hers. "Lady Grace, I owe you a great debt of gratitude for all your work these past few days," she said. "Here you are, only a Maid of Honour and not yet of age. Yet, with the help of your good friends here, you have saved Sir Charles's life, unearthed the wickedness of his brother, and discovered the poisoner of Sir Gerald. There are many men in my employ who have done far less and with less difficulty in their path. Be sure I shall make a good grant to you and find a more worthy guardian to take care of it."

I nodded. "I could help you if there were any more mysteries at Court, too," I whispered.

The Queen laughed. The she whispered back in my ear, "You shall be my first Lady Pursuivant. Let wrongdoers beware!"

I was thrilled! A pursuivant is someone who pursues wrongdoers for the Crown, though most pursuivants mainly pursue spies and assassins. It was all so exciting!

"But have a care, Grace," warned the Queen with a tiny frown. "I still expect my Maid of Honour to behave as befits her blood. I will have no more wild trips down the river at night . . . unless *absolutely* necessary. . . ."

"No, Your Majesty," I said meekly.

Then she smiled again, and clasped me, and sent me to my chamber while Mrs. Bea made me a hot posset to help me sleep (which I haven't drunk yet and it's gone cold). Mary Shelton brought it for me and gave me some of her delicious almond bisket bread. I never realized before how kind she is. And even Lady Sarah is being less trying than usual. I feel very strange about being poor all of a sudden, but I had to stop again. It was Sir Charles and Dr. Cavendish come to visit me.

Sir Charles was looking, and smelling, much better—he was clean and had shaved and his black eye had ointment on it. "Lady Grace," he said, "is it true what I hear of how Lord Worthy wasted your estates?"

I nodded a little dolefully. "But the Queen will help me and she said she would never send me away."

"My dear Lady Greensleeves," said Sir Charles, "were you aware that when there has been a murder, all the murderer's money and property goes to the nearest relative of the victim?"

I nodded. Yes, I'd heard that. But why did that concern me?

"Well," Sir Charles continued, "I am Sir Gerald's heir. His father was my mother's cousin. Which means that I shall inherit Lord Worthy's estates."

I stared. I was really too tired to follow this. "You?"

"Yes," Sir Charles confirmed. "And Lord Worthy's estates are, I am sure, worth more than yours ever were—despite his being a poor manager of his affairs. I, however, am not and I am already wealthy enough for my needs." He took a deep breath. "I shall see my lawyer tomorrow and when all the necessary paperwork has been done, I shall make all I get from Lord Worthy over to you, in recompense for what Lord Worthy misused."

"You will?" I gasped.

He nodded, looking very bright-eyed.

"But why?" I burst out.

Sir Charles smiled fondly at me. "My dear, I know you do not love me, yet for justice's sake you saved my very life. How can I do other than see you do not lose by it?"

So there it is. Sir Charles Amesbury will give me Lord Worthy's estates and even redeem what he can of my own lands. And he said he would petition the Queen to be my guardian and keep good care of them. So from being poor as a church mouse, I am rich again!

Maybe one day I *shall* marry—but it will be for love. My mother always said she loved my father and it was the best of marriages, though it was cut short.

For now? I remain Lady Grace Cavendish, Maid of Honour—and secret Lady Pursuivant! I know that my mother would be proud of that. And *I* cannot think of anything that could make me happier!

GLOSSARY

addled—confused, muddled, spoiled

agrimony—an herb

aiglet—the metal tip of a lace on a garment, which you thread through holes

Allah—the Muslim name for God

apothecary—an Elizabethan chemist

aqua vitae—brandy

Bedlam—the major asylum for the insane in London during Elizabethan times—the name came from the Hospital of St. Mary of Bethlehem

bezoar stone—a hard, stonelike object from a goat's stomach, used by Elizabethans (unsuccessfully) to cure poisoning

birch—to beat (birch twigs were often used)

blackwork—black embroidery on white linen

Board of Green Cloth—the main administrative body for the Court. It dealt with an inquest if anyone died within one mile of the Queen's person.

bodice—the top part of a woman's dress

borage—an herb

Boy King—King Edward VI, Elizabeth's brother, who died young

brocade—a rich, gold-embroidered fabric

bum—bottom

bumroll—a sausage-shaped piece of padding worn round the hips to make them look bigger

canions—showy fabric leggings, a little like shorts, worn by men

casket—a small decorative box

cinnabar—a red compound of mercury and sulfur, used as red coloring for lips, cheeks, painting, etc.

City Fathers—the rulers of the City of London

close-stool—a portable toilet comprising a seat with a hole in it on top of a box with a chamber pot inside

cloth of estate—a kind of awning that went over the Queen's chair to indicate that she was the monarch

cloth of silver/gold—cloth woven from silk thread that had been wrapped in fine gold or silver wire

commoner—anyone who did not hold the rank of gentleman or higher and therefore did not have a coat of arms

crayfish—a shellfish a little like a lobster but smaller

damask—a beautiful, self-patterned silk cloth woven in Flanders. It originally came from Damascus—hence the name.

daybooke—a book in which you would record your sins each day so that you could pray about them. The idea of keeping a diary or journal grew out of this. Grace uses her daybooke as a journal.

djinni—an Arabic word for a mischievous spirit—also known as a djinn or genie

doublet—a close-fitting padded jacket worn by men

dugs—breasts

eringo—sea holly, a plant that grows by the sea. It was eaten pickled or candied and thought to have some medicinal properties as well as being a food.

false front—a pretty piece of material sewn to the front of a plain petticoat so that it would show under the kirtle

farthingale—a bell- or barrel-shaped petticoat held out with hoops of whalebone

Grace-and-Favour Chambers—rooms provided to important courtiers by the Queen

Guise—the House of Guise, which was the royal family of France

handfasted—formally engaged to be married

harlot—a prostitute

hose—tight-fitting cloth trousers worn by men

hoyden—a tomboy

Huguenots—French Christians who followed the Protestant, rather than the Roman Catholic, Church

kirtle—the skirt of an Elizabethan dress

kohl—black eye makeup

Lady Dowager mother—a widow who retains the title "Lady" even though her husband's title has passed to his son and heir

Lady Hoby—one of the Queen's favorite Ladies-in-Waiting

Lady-in-Waiting—one of the ladies who helped to look after the Queen and kept her company

laudanum—an opium tincture in alcohol used to aid sleep

Lord Chamberlain—the man in charge of security and entertainment at court

lye—an ingredient in soap. It is strongly alkaline and was used for cleaning.

lying at—sleeping at

lying-in chamber—a room where a woman would give birth

madrigals—beautiful part-songs, which were very fashionable

Maid of Honour—a younger girl who helped to look after the Queen like a Lady-in-Waiting

manchet rolls—whole wheat bread

marchpane subtlety—a sculpture made out of marzipan and then colored

marmelada—a very thick jammy sweet often made from quinces

marten—fur from a marten, a small carnivorous animal

Mary Shelton—one of Queen Elizabeth's Maids of Honor (a Maid of Honor of this name really did exist; see below). Most Maids of Honor were not officially "Ladies" (like Lady Grace), but they had to be born of gentry.

mead—an alcoholic drink made with honey

megrim—a migraine headache

Mr. Rackmaster Norton—the torturer

Papist—a rude word for a Catholic

Paris Garden—an Elizabethan leisure garden beside the Thames that featured all kinds of entertainments

partlet—a very fine embroidered false top that covered just the shoulders and the upper chest

pate—head

pattens—wooden clogs worn to keep fine shoes out of the mud *penner*—a small leather case that would attach to a belt. It was used for holding quills, ink, knife, and any other equipment needed for writing.

pennyroyal mint—an herb

plague—a virulent disease that killed thousands

poignard—an extremely sharp, long, thin blade sometimes used for dueling

posset—a hot drink made from sweetened and spiced milk curdled with ale or wine

potherbs—vegetables

Presence Chamber—the room where Queen Elizabeth would receive people

Privy Garden—Queen Elizabeth's private garden

Privy Parlour—Queen Elizabeth's private parlor

pulses—the beats of the heart

pursuivant—a follower or attendant who pursues someone else

Queen's Guard—more commonly known as the Gentlemen Pensioners—young noblemen who guarded the Queen from physical attacks

religious wars—conflicts arising from religious differences

sallet—salad

scurvy—an affliction brought on by lack of vitamin C in the diet

Secretary Cecil—William Cecil, an administrator for the Queen (later made Lord Burghley)

Shaitan—the Islamic word for Satan, though it means a trickster and a liar rather than the ultimate evil

shift—a polite name for a smock

sippet—a piece of bread, buttered and lightly grilled, from which meat was eaten. The sippet soaked up the meat juices.

smallpox—a nasty, often fatal disease, whose pustules healed and left scars

smock—a neck-to-ankles linen shirt worn by women

staging stable—a stable where horses were kept temporarily when on the way to somewhere else

stays—the boned, laced bodice worn around the body under the clothes. Victorians called the stays a corset.

stews—public baths

Stone Gallery—a passageway at the Palace of Whitehall that led to the Queen's chambers

strumpet—a prostitute

sucket—a sweet

sugar plate—sugar candy that could be molded like modeling clay, then dried and colored

sweetmeats—sweets

tansy—an herb

tides of the blood—the Elizabethans believed that the blood flowed in tides in the body, like the sea.

Tilting Yard—an area where knights in armor would joust or tilt (i.e., ride at each other on horseback with lances)

tincture—a solution of a substance in alcohol

tinder box—a small box containing some quick-burning tinder, a piece of flint, a piece of steel, and a candle for making fire and thus light

tiring woman—a woman who helped a lady to dress

toothcloth—a coarse cloth, often beautifully embroidered, used for rubbing teeth clean

truckle bed—a small bed on wheels stored under the main bed

tumbler—an acrobat

Verge of the Court—anywhere within a mile of the Queen's person

virginals—an instrument, similar to a harpsichord, played by Queen Elizabeth

vomitus—vomit (noun)

watch candle—a night-light

watersteps—steps leading down to the river Thames

wherry—a Thames boat

white lead—lead carbonate, used for white paint and makeup

Withdrawing Chamber—the Queen's private rooms

A NOTE ABOUT POISONS . . .

Darkwort is not a real poison. It was invented for this story. However, there are plenty of real poisons that are similar to darkwort and that come from trees, plants, and flowers commonly found in our parks and gardens. Since the Elizabethans relied upon the plants around them for medicines and cleaning chemicals, as well as food, they were far more familiar with poisonous plants than we are today.

A NOTE ABOUT APPAREL . . .

Apparel (clothing) in Elizabethan times was incredibly expensive. Even ordinary clothes were costly because a great deal of labor was involved in making them (spinning, dyeing, weaving, hand-sewing, etc.). Court clothes were very richly decorated and made from the finest fabrics—often costing as much as an expensive sports car would today.

Poor people would probably have an old second-hand outfit; ordinary people would have just one secondhand suit, and rich people might have two or three outfits. Ridiculously wealthy people would have ten or twenty outfits and would show off by making them extravagantly elaborate.

Have you ever heard the story of Sir Walter Raleigh laying his cloak over a puddle for Queen Elizabeth to step on? That was rather like driving a brand-new Ferrari into a tree in order to impress Madonna!

In 1485, Queen Elizabeth I's grandfather, Henry Tudor, won the battle of Bosworth Field against Richard III and took the throne of England. He was known as Henry VII. He had two sons, Arthur and Henry. Arthur died while still a boy, so when Henry VII died in 1509, Elizabeth's father came to the throne and England got an eighth king called Henry—the notorious one who had six wives.

Wife number one—Catherine of Aragon—gave Henry one daughter called Mary (who was brought up as a Catholic) but no living sons. To Henry VIII this was a disaster, because nobody believed a queen could ever govern England. He needed a male heir.

Henry wanted to divorce Catherine so he could marry his pregnant mistress, Anne Boleyn. The Pope, the head of the Catholic Church, wouldn't allow him to annul his marriage, so Henry broke with the Catholic Church and set up the Protestant Church of England—or the Episcopal Church, as it's known in the United States.

Wife number two—Anne Boleyn—gave Henry another daughter, Elizabeth (who was brought up as a Protestant). When Anne then miscarried a baby boy, Henry decided he'd better get somebody new, so he accused Anne of infidelity and had her executed.

Wife number three—Jane Seymour—gave Henry a son called Edward and died of childbed fever a couple of weeks later.

Wife number four—Anne of Cleves—had no children. It was a diplomatic marriage and Henry didn't fancy her, so she agreed to a divorce (wouldn't you?).

Wife number five—Catherine Howard—had no children, either. Like Anne Boleyn, she was accused of infidelity and executed.

Wife number six—Catherine Parr—also had no children. She did manage to outlive Henry, though, but only by the skin of her teeth. Nice guy, eh?

Henry VIII died in 1547, and in accordance with the rules of primogeniture (whereby the firstborn son inherits from his father), the person who succeeded him was the boy Edward. He became Edward VI. He was strongly Protestant but died young, in 1553.

Next came Catherine of Aragon's daughter, Mary, who became Mary I, known as Bloody Mary. She was strongly Catholic, married Philip II of Spain in a diplomatic match, but died childless five years later. She also burned a lot of Protestants for the good of their souls.

Finally, in 1558, Elizabeth came to the throne. She reigned until her death in 1603. She played the marriage game—that is, she kept a lot of important and influential men hanging on in hopes of marrying her—for a long time. At one time it looked as if she would marry her favorite, Robert Dudley, Earl of Leicester. She didn't, though, and I think she probably never intended to get married—would you, if you'd had a dad like hers? So she never had any children.

She was an extraordinary and brilliant woman, and during her reign, England first started to become important as a world power. Sir Francis Drake sailed round the world—raiding the Spanish colonies of South America for loot as he went. And one of

Elizabeth's favorite courtiers, Sir Walter Raleigh, tried to plant the first English colony in North America—at the site of Roanoke in 1585. It failed, but the idea stuck.

The Spanish King Philip II tried to conquer England in 1588. He sent a huge fleet of 150 ships, known as the Invincible Armada, to do it. It failed miserably—defeated by Drake at the head of the English fleet—and most of the ships were wrecked trying to sail home. There were many other great Elizabethans, too—including William Shakespeare and Christopher Marlowe.

After her death, Elizabeth was succeeded by James VI of Scotland, who became James I of England and Scotland. He was almost the last eligible person available! He was the son of Mary, Queen of Scots, who was Elizabeth's cousin, via Henry VIII's sister.

James's son was Charles I—the king who was beheaded after losing the English Civil War.

The stories about Lady Grace Cavendish are set in the year 1569, when Elizabeth was thirty-six and still playing the marriage game for all she was worth. The Ladies-in-Waiting and Maids of Honor at her

Court weren't servants—they were companions and friends, supplied from upper-class families. Not all of them were officially "Ladies"—only those with titled husbands or fathers; in fact, many of them were unmarried younger daughters sent to Court to find themselves a nice rich lord to marry.

All the Lady Grace Mysteries are invented, but some of the characters in the stories are real people—Queen Elizabeth herself, of course, and Mrs. Champernowne and Mary Shelton as well. There never was a Lady Grace Cavendish (as far as we know!)—but there were plenty of girls like her at Elizabeth's Court. The real Mary Shelton foolishly made fun of the Queen herself on one occasion—and got slapped in the face by Elizabeth for her trouble! But most of the time, the Queen seems to have been protective of and kind to her Maids of Honor. She was very strict about boyfriends, though. There was one simple rule for boyfriends in those days: you couldn't have one. No boyfriends at all. You would get married to a person your parents chose for you and that was that. Of course, the girls often had other ideas!

Later on in her reign, the Queen had a full-scale secret service run by her great spymaster, Sir

Francis Walsingham. His men, who hunted down priests and assassins, were called Pursuivants. There are also tantalizing hints that Elizabeth may have had her own personal sources of information—she certainly was very well informed, even when her counselors tried to keep her in the dark. And who knows whom she might have recruited to find things out for her? There may even have been a Lady Grace Cavendish, after all!

Be on the lookout

for the next

Lady Grace Mystery,

BETRAYAL,

on sale now!